ANGELINA'S LIPS

PROSE SERIES 89

Guernica Editions gratefully acknowledge the John Fowles Center for Creative Writing, the Musco Chair in Italian Studies, Wilkinson College, Chapman University, and the Istituto Italiano di Cultura di Los Angeles for help in the organization of the Italian Writers Series of 2009 that paved the way for the realization of the present publication.

GIUSEPPE CONTE

ANGELINA'S LIPS

TRANSLATED BY ROBERT BURANELLO

EDITED BY MARK AXELROD

GUERNICA
Toronto·Buffalo·Lancaster (U.K.)
2011

Mark Axelrod, editor
Guernica Editions Inc.
P.O. Box 117, Station P, Toronto (ON), Canada M5S 2S6
2250 Military Road, Tonawanda, N.Y. 14150-6000 U.S.A.

Distributors:
University of Toronto Press Distribution,
5201 Dufferin Street, Toronto (ON), Canada M3H 5T8
Gazelle Book Services, White Cross Mills, High Town, Lancaster LA1 4XS U.K.

First edition.
Printed in Canada.

Legal Deposit – Third Quarter
Library of Congress Catalog Card Number:
Library and Archives Canada Cataloguing in Publication
Conte, Giuseppe, 1945-
Angelina's lips / Giuseppe Conte ; translated by Robert Buranello.
(Prose series ; 89)
Translation of: I personaggi dei romanzi futuri.
Text in English and Italian.
ISBN 978-1-55071-337-4
I. Buranello, Robert, 1964- II. Title.
III. Series: Prose series ; 89.
PQ4863.O4837P4713 2011   853'.914   C2010-907176-X

CONTENTS

PREFACE

The idea for creating the John Fowles Center for Creative Writing came to me while I was on a Leverhulme Fellowship at the University of East Anglia, Norwich, UK in 1996. While there, I met Christopher Bigsby who was the director of the Arthur Miller Centre for American Studies. It wasn't a "centre" as such since it was housed in Bigsby's office, but among other things the centre did was to invite a number of authors (local or otherwise as long as they were accessible by train) to come to UEA, read from their work and be interviewed by Bigsby. I thought the idea was engaging and, because of my long standing friendship with the late John Fowles, I asked him, while on a visit to Lyme Regis, if I could use his name and organize something similar at Chapman University, but devoted to creative writing. "Anything for creative writing students," Fowles said, and, in 1997, I initiated the first series by inviting the Argentine novelist, Luisa Valenzuela.

The center has grown significantly since then and 2011 marks the fourteenth year for the John Fowles Center. Over those fourteen years, the center has hosted such notable inter/national authors as: Salman Rushdie, Nobel Laureate Wole Soyinka, David Antin, Fanny Howe,

Carlos Fuentes, Maxine Hong Kingston, John Ashbery, Lawrence Ferlinghetti, Charles Bernstein, Willis Barnstone, Elias Khoury and a host of other accomplished writers. Sometimes the series was devoted to specific kinds of writers: Latin American writers or "experimental writers" or poets or Arab and Jewish writers. But, in 2009, I decided to devote the entire series to Italian writers or those of Italian heritage. I invited the Italian-American novelist, Tony Ardizzone; the Italian-Canadian poet, Pasquale Verdicchio; and four Italian writers, Francesca Duranti, Dacia Maraini, Giorgio Pressburger, and, of course, Giuseppe Conte. I invited Conte based on the suggestion of a friend of mine who had read his work in Italian and, since the majority of the Italians I invited were writing prose, Conte's poetry would strike a poetic balance. I read a copy of *The Ocean and the Boy (L'oceano e il ragazzo)* and was not only struck by the effusiveness of Calvino's introductory praise for the book, but that the poems reflect how civilizations pay homage to the natural world which is at the forefront of all his lyricality. For Conte, man is inextricably connected to the earth.

After his arrival in Los Angeles, I picked him up at the Best Western Sunset Plaza Hotel located in West Hollywood and drove him back to Orange County. At the time, I didn't think much about the hotel though I recall the lobby and the architecture had a distinctly '40s kind of feel to it. Something Nathanael West may have thought about as he was writing *Day of the Locust.* As we drove back to Orange County, Conte complained about his English not being good enough to read his poetry and said he would feel more comfortable if he could read in Italian and have someone translate in English. My colleague at Chapman, Italianist Robert Buranello, was eager to do just that and, at the evening reading, Conte read brilliantly and Buranello's interpretation of the poetry was flawless. Subsequent to the reading, many of my students told me that Conte's reading was one of the best if not the best of the entire Italian series and that the reading was one of the best they had heard of all the readings they had been to.

The day before Conte left, I drove him to Laguna Beach for a breakfast. Knowing his unmitigated love of nature and the sea, I thought that, perhaps, Laguna Beach might "inspire" him in some way. Of course, since he lives in Sanremo, it wasn't as if he were barren of natural inspiration, but I thought it would be a different kind of inspiration since Laguna Beach is unique in its own rather multifarious bourgeois way. We had a pleasant breakfast at the Café Zinc and walked along the Laguna Beach boardwalk for about an hour discussing many things in general and nothing in particular. From my perspective, it didn't seem as if Conte were that impressed with Laguna Beach and its natives. It wasn't as if he were attracted by anything in particular. A day later, he returned to Italy.

Not long after his visit, Conte emailed me and thanked me for hosting him and I told him it was a pleasure and that I looked forward to inviting him again. A few months later, he sent me an email with an attachment. When I opened the attachment I discovered the story, *I personaggi dei romanzi futuri* with the additional line, "Dovuto a Mark Axelrod". Needless to say, I was moved by the gesture since it was the last thing I expected. I immediately sent a copy to Robert Buranello with the suggestion that the two of us should collaborate on a translation of the story with the possibility of publication. And so we did. With the assistance of Pasquale Verdicchio and Michael Mirolla of Guernica, Conte's story has now been published.

But I'd like to say a few things about the story itself since it was clearly influenced by Conte's stay in Southern California and not insignificantly his visit to Laguna Beach. The story, which has been re-titled as *Angelina's Lips*, is based upon the main character, Umberto Umber, and his obsession with... well... Angelina Jolie's lips. To be Hitchcockian about it, the story deals with the relationship between Umber, a professor of comparative literature, and a Dr. Jamshid Kloster, an experimental physicist whom Umber meets on a Laguna Beach bench as Diane Keaton, a long-time Laguna Beach resident, strolls by. Apparently, Conte wasn't as oblivious to his Laguna Beach surroundings as I thought he was.

Umber's other obsession or, perhaps, his deepest regret is that as time goes by he will never be able to know any of "the characters of future novels." In Hitchcockian terms, that's the McGuffin and as Kloster tells Umber: "If you're interested in future novels, we must travel to the libraries of the future." And that's where the story becomes both Borgesian and Contesque as Umber asks

Kloster what he will need for that to happen and Kloster replies: "We need a library, four mirrors, and a beautiful sunset." That said, I take my exit from this preface and leave you with Angelina's lips, Umber's obsessions, Kloster's physics, a library, four mirrors, a beautiful sunset and Diane Keaton strolling somewhere on the sands of Laguna Beach.

Mark Axelrod
Somewhere near,
but not quite on, Laguna Beach
September, 2010

ANGELINA'S LIPS

For Mark Axelrod

Somewhere in his hippyish youth, Umberto Umber had read that California is situated at the bottom of an inclined plane and that whatever is not well-rooted tumbles down. Having arrived at an advanced age and always feeling totally free of any kind of attachment, rather than tumble down there, he chose to slide blithely into a position at a California university and a home in Laguna Beach where, despite the distance of thousands of kilometres, it seems like being in a more extensive and tranquil Côte d'Azur. Professor Umber had no real ties to anything tangible. He was Italian, even if in Italy his name led people to believe that he was a foreigner. There or abroad, many colleagues poked fun at the striking similarity between his name and that of the protagonist of that very famous twentieth-century novel. He would patiently smile while noting that he lacked two "h"s and an extra "t" in order to be the namesake of that character in *Lolita*.

With a mischievous glance, he would also add that he had never had a thing for young girls. This was true. He had never been tempted by any of his students. He had never had lovers. He had been married to an energetic and strong-willed woman, a lawyer who earned ten times what he did. The marriage ended after a few years, and so sweetly that he could not even remember the reason why. He considered himself fortunate since, based on the experiences of so many of his colleagues, he knew what kinds of mental and financial devastation a divorce can bring. He owned no property. His parents, whom he had lost early in life, left him an apartment and some investments. He had sold everything.

After the divorce, he always rented furnished apartments, reducing to the bare minimum what he would have to transport with each move. All he needed was an apartment with two rooms. If it was near a port, better still. He was a professor of comparative literature and he would find the books he needed for his work in the libraries of the universities that would hire him to teach. This way, Umberto Umber moved around light as a feather. Even his wardrobe was reduced to the essentials: a few jackets, lots of t-shirts and shirts, jeans, loafers. That was enough in California. He was staying in the hills of Laguna Beach, on that particular hill that the fires occasionally ravage, but at a reasonable distance – a mere stroll – from the beach of fine ivory sand in front of the open ocean.

He had kept his European habits. He would walk down to have breakfast in a café where he would drink a cappuccino with a muffin or croissant while leafing through the *Los Angeles Times* in search of curious news items. In the evening he would dine at a restaurant where, by now, all the waiters knew him and would greet him with a handshake when he arrived and when he left. He would eat some kind of lavish salad with shrimp or turkey accompanied by a glass of red wine. He was a man whose life was of no importance to anyone. There was no woman who loved him, nor did he feel the need for one. He had students, male and female, but it was evident that they did not need him for their studies. He had many acquaintances, but not one true friend.

In the end, he wouldn't have known what to share with a friend. He wouldn't even know what to discuss since he wasn't interested in anything. In his opinion, the academic life, politics, sports, economics held no attraction at all. He didn't allow himself to be overwhelmed by memories, despite his advanced age. No nostalgia bound him to Italy where he was born and raised, nor to France where he had taught for a number of years, nor to his youth. Drifting into California was natural for him since no attachment held him back. So, there he was, in front of the immeasurable vastness of the Pacific. Toward evening, he would go out again and stay a long while along the ocean front, among the gardens, boardwalks, and benches, then he would go down to the beach and gaze into the horizon. Beyond the horizon, there was Asia, the rising sun. He was feeling good there, in the twilight.

***

If it is true that Professor Umber had no real ties to anything tangible, this does not mean that he had no ties at all. He did, and how! But with beings whose lives manifest themselves in the world of imagination, with beings who are the most concrete and vibrant forms of unreality. He had ties to characters in books, poems and novels that he had read about over the course of his existence and for which he developed an unhealthy love consisting of fantasies and further fictions. As an obscure scholar, he published the minimum that would allow him to continue an equally obscure academic career. The fact is that, as opposed to a more analytical relationship whose importance and heroic grandeur he did recognize, he preferred a licentious love affair with literary characters straight away. It was a weakness and he knew it. Perhaps even an embarrassment. But there was nothing he could do about it.

Like so many adolescents, he had fallen in love with the images of the great divas of the day, especially Gina Lollobrigida and Marilyn Monroe. With the former, he had imagined brief encounters in the back of a Rolls Royce, fervid kisses on stupendously drawn lips, and a neck and breasts as white as pure flour, snow, sugar. When as an older man he crossed paths with the already aged diva in an airport, it was still the absolute whiteness of her skin that struck him. With the latter, it had been something else entirely – a real love story. He had danced with her better than Yves Montand in *Let's Make Love*;

he'd kissed her better than Tony Curtis in *Some Like it Hot*; he'd spoken to her better than Arthur Miller that evening he grasped her big toe between his fingers and began seducing her at a party. He immersed himself in her carnality, to resurface as pure spirit. He loved her as if he had had her right there, in his room, as a boy, all for himself. When he received the news of her suicide, it seemed as if he had lost a part of his world, the most innocent and unhealthy.

However, in that same period there began to stir in him the first signs of love that, different from the first, few if any would have experienced. As a boy, Umber began to isolate the characters from the pages of his books and to fantasize about them, dream of them, spend hours and hours of his day with them. Then, he just carried on with it. It was his secret, his incurable disease. The young Princess Nausicaa of the *Odyssey* captured his imagination. As if Homer's verses were not enough, in his folly Umber added little touches of color to the character. He imagined her hairstyle, gait, garments, and more: her lips, hands, breasts, thighs.

There were no limits to his audacity and his longing. Without the least respect, he lifted Francesca da Rimini from the *Divine Comedy* and, taking the place of Paolo, he repeatedly relived the adulterous act with her after that book of love had inspired them to look into each other's eyes, making them turn pale, sweat, and tremble to death. For years he was the boyfriend of Rosalind, the main character of *As You Like It*. That was what he liked: a girl, as Shakespeare knew how to imagine her, in a concealing outfit, wandering in the Forest of Arden with such a natural allure that no disguise could diminish it. Then, he was in love with Ottilie, the character from *Elective Affinities*. He shared her thoughts, her pains; he was constantly moved to tears by the chemical inevitability of her fate.

Umber posed no limits on himself. Between Frollo and Quasimodo, Phoebus and Gringoire, he allowed himself to be seduced by Esméralda, the fatally beautiful gypsy of *The Hunchback of Notre Dame*. He wandered through the woods of the Friuli and the quays of Venice with la Pisana of *Confessions of an Italian*. He burst the banks of propriety with Connie Chatterley. He not only had breakfast with Holly Golightly at Tiffany's, but at all the best jewellery shops and restaurants in New York, Paris and London. There is no need to believe that these affairs were exclusively sexual. Umber would fall in love with the woman only if he considered her a well-written character.

As he got older, he also frequently fell in love with male characters. Although the catalogue of conquests would be too long to list, he certainly had affairs with Robinson Crusoe, Tristram Shandy, Fra Cristoforo, David Copperfield, Jean Valjean, Ahab, Captain Nemo, Jim Hawkins, Sherlock Holmes, Andrei Bolkonski, Dick Diver, Leopold Bloom, Cosimo Piovasco di Rondò and many, many others. When he had a character in his head with whom he could interact and with whom imagine new adventures, he was never alone. These were the relationships that gave meaning to his life, that filled it at times with boundless joy – absurd yet undeniable – of which he was almost ashamed.

You can probably imagine the discomfort that would seize Professor Umberto Umber when he heard his more academically respected colleagues debate the "death of the novel." For him, the death of the novel meant the death of a troupe of characters he lived with, the death of a part of himself. Luckily for him, these theories were less prevalent in California. So, while walking by the ocean at Laguna Beach, he could continue to ponder how he could have saved Esméralda from Frollo's vile dagger, or to imagine a fifty-something Connie Chatterley betraying Mellors with a young aristocrat. Why not?

***

When, on certain mornings, Umberto Umber would see his neighbor Diane Keaton run along the ocean front, it wasn't her he was following with his eyes, but Woody Allen's muse, or the star of that extraordinarily fun and sexy film with Jack Nicholson about mature love, whose title he couldn't recall. Once again, it was the character that got the upper hand on the real person. The actresses he preferred in this late stage of his life were Angelina Jolie and Jennifer Lopez. The former, so tall and thin yet adaptable, with that cold, post-human face dominated by those lips that appeared to be of a material other than flesh, seemed to him like a model of women of the future. The latter was of the present: complete sweetness, round, full of life in the here and now, like a calm river that flows confidently between its banks, certain to reach the sea. Jennifer Lopez – if he could have, he would have chosen her as star of the Latino heavens. Voice, color, radiance, ass – everything about her attracted him without, of course, the upsetting issues of adolescence.

When Umber would have coffee at 8600 Sunset Boulevard in West Hollywood, he used to enjoy strolling with the sun at his back down to where Sunset intersects with La Cienega Boulevard that, despite the occasional asymmetrical swerve, descends steep and straight in the direction of the sea. His glance seemed not to follow a street but a canyon cut into the living body of a city. When he returned from there late at night, he stood spellbound by the sight of La Cienega Boulevard covered by a stream of lava in one direction and very dense sparkles of golden starlight in the other. He would arrive at the neo-gothic and slightly absurd turreted silhouette of the Chateau Marmont whose rooms had been home to so many actresses and actors who had lent their likenesses to characters that had inspired the dreams of the greatest audiences in the world. Umber thought of Clark Gable in *Gone With the Wind*, William Holden in *Love is a Many-Splendored Thing*.

However, what was very strange was that the film characters affected him less than those from novels to whom he could add the body and the voice that he preferred, contributing to their re-creation with his own, personal imagination. So, while strolling there, between 8600 and 8200 Sunset Boulevard, Umber was thinking of Angelina Jolie and Jennifer Lopez but he realized right away that, if instead of being real women in flesh (Jennifer) and bone (Angelina) and Hollywood stars, they had been the main characters in some novel, if he had discovered them in the pages of some book, he would have liked them much, much more. This was a sickness for which Umber had no name yet he was aware of being afflicted by it. Not only did he not want to recover from it, but he experienced a subtle and melancholic pleasure in knowing that it was getting worse as the years passed and that this passion of his was becoming a kind of sweet madness.

As a scholar and reader, Umber knew everything about the characters in novels already written, published, and listed in literary histories. Yet this particular madness caused him to torment himself over knowing absolutely nothing about those characters that are still to come, that would be added, that would be the focus of those novels that are about to occupy the windows of bookshops and the bookshelves of libraries around the world. As time passed and as the aches and pains of age set in (the nights he had difficulty falling asleep, the two or three times a night he would have to get out of bed to pee, the days when the sharp pain in his right knee would keep him from walking on the beach), the thought of never knowing even one of the characters from the novels of the future began to obsess him. By taking more care of his health through regular check-ups on his blood pressure and his cholesterol levels, avoiding smoking – even his pipe that he always enjoyed so much, eliminating animal fats from his diet, limiting his alcohol intake to that one glass of wine (whereas before he used to indulge in more than a bit of whiskey and cognac), taking the necessary dietary supplements, doing what little physical exercise his congenital laziness and that rheumatism he developed would permit, he could hope to live another twenty years or so. Another twenty years in which novelists' imaginations would invent new characters that he would get to know, evaluate, follow, interrogate, bring back to life.

Then what? In his inoffensive but nonetheless alarming madness, this was the aspect of death that worried and upset him most: that he wouldn't be able to know more about the new Emma Bovarys and which new Père Goriots were out there, and not even the new Miss Marples and Maigrets that would appear on the literary horizon. This was intolerable to him. Yet, he thought about it again and again, continuously. But what remedy could he ever find to something that presented itself to him with the unavoidability of the laws of nature and the destiny all mortals share?

***

Umberto Umber certainly was not inclined to dwell on his own personal immortality. A consciousness that extended beyond the confines of his own existence was enough for him. He realized that he was asking a lot but it wasn't as if he was presuming to compete with God, immortal by definition. Whatever is born also dies, thought Umber, with full resignation to his typical condition of being born of woman. But how did the characters in novels – the great characters – born of men and women as well, manage to transcend centuries and millennia? How can we still be moved and frustrated by them? Fail, laugh, travel, tremble, run, and love with them? There is a mystery to this superhuman existence, a spark of the divine that exists in them, Umberto Umber was telling himself as he was becoming more and more obsessed with these thoughts.

One morning along the Laguna Beach boardwalk, he noticed a man for the first time. On a bench next to his, a grey-haired lady dressed in an elegant white tracksuit was meditating in the lotus position; on another, two young girls sitting very close to each other – one in black jeans and jacket, the other in a short skirt and colorful blouse – who, between giggles, were independently talking on their cell phones. Despite all this, the man seated on the middle bench, who seemed to be Umber's age, never turned to look at them. He was neither annoyed nor curious. From the way he was dressed – a light, wrinkled corduroy jacket, cotton pants, sandals, and his face – tortoise-shell glasses, a slightly unkempt grey beard, one would think he was a professor too. The combination of his rather dark complexion and deep, black eyes revealed his Asian origins. He could have been Indian, Pakistani, or Iranian – it wasn't easy to tell which. He was reading the *Los Angeles Times* and every once in a while he would slowly sip from a paper cup some liquid that must have been coffee.

Suddenly, Umber made one of those instinctive decisions that baffle the senses themselves and went to sit on that particular bench, right next to the stranger. He also began to read the newspaper and the two men stayed that way – side-by-side, and more alike than their skin colors would reveal – for almost an hour. Diane Keaton passed by that morning too, and neither man had anything to say about it.

***

The following day Umber found the man on the same bench. Even the lady who was meditating in the lotus position dutifully returned to the bench next to theirs. Umber took a seat. The two men sat silently next to each other for a long time. Umber suspected that he did not speak English. Then he remembered the *Los Angeles Times* that he had in his hands the day before. He ruled out the possibility that he was only looking at the photographs. Umber was stealing quick, discreet glances in his direction. He did not want to be noticed.

He was intrigued by that man, by that almost priestly, absorbed demeanor, by that rapt stillness. Perhaps he is not a professor, Umber said to himself while thinking of his loquacious, quick-witted, malicious and gossipy colleagues. So, who was he, then? An unemployed screenwriter? A retired doctor? Another person who tumbled to California because he hadn't managed to lay down roots anywhere else? Then he asked a generic yet legitimate question that popped into his head. Taking advantage of the fact that the stranger had just been distracted from his thoughts and shifted his glance to Umber's direction, he enquired: "Have you been living here for a long time?"

"That depends on what you mean by 'a long time'," replied the stranger.

Umber was struck by the wisdom of those words. He quickly said: "I've been here for less than a year."

"For me, it's been less than a month," said the stranger with a smile. He revealed a row of perfectly aligned yet yellowed teeth like those of avid smokers. "My name is Kloster."

Umber wondered how he could have been so wrong. This man he had indisputably judged to be Asian was actually German.

Having noticed Umber's amazement, the stranger continued: "I am Dr. Jamshid Kloster. I was born in Germany to a German father and an Iranian mother, may Allah bless her soul. I am here to continue my studies. I work on the correlation between time and light."

Umber was confused. He thought it would be too indiscreet to ask if he was Muslim.

"So, you're a professor?"

"No, I'm a researcher. I don't teach."

Umber's bewilderment increased. A researcher. Why, then, was he sitting on that bench and not in a laboratory? Why did he not have a briefcase full of books and files? Why just a casually tossed canvas bag from which the neck of a bottle of mineral water and a crumpled copy of the *Los Angeles Times* peeped out?

***

If not quite a friendship, at least a certain familiarity developed between Umber and Kloster. After breakfast, they would meet at the Oceanside and stroll along a stretch of beach. Now Umber would also bring with him a cup of coffee or a bottle of mineral water, sometimes muffins or chocolate sweets that he would regularly offer Kloster who would always decline. They talked of nothing personal; nothing regarding their past lives in Europe. It seemed like an unspoken agreement. Very unspoken. Each of them had only divulged a few generalities and some information about their professions. A German with an Iranian mother; an Italian who had taught in France; a researcher in physics; a professor of comparative literature.

Whoever saw them walking together on the pale golden sand of Laguna Beach would have easily mistaken them for aged hippies from who-knows-where, who grew old still following their dreams. Their discussions primarily focussed on what they had just read in the *Los Angeles Times*. They would not dwell on politics too much, even if they were both supporters of the new President Barack Hussein Obama. They loved his manner, expressions, ideas, and they agreed with his first measures to combat the crisis into which America had fallen. Neither of them would dwell on the country's economic conditions though they would laughingly comment on never seeing American cars in the US, a country designed to be seen on four wheels – complete with drive-in cinemas, drive-thru restaurants and even churches – that had allowed its automobile industry to go belly-up and had to be replenished by the Germans and Japanese against whom they had spent so much energy fighting in the Second World War. They would discuss news items more willingly: sea storms with gigantic waves, fires in the hills, homicides downtown, bloody robberies in Beverly Hills mansions, or reviews of the latest films like the one by Clint Eastwood or the latest novel by Patricia Cornwell. Then, eventually, the discussion would shift to the projects on which they were working.

Umber talked about his lectures at the university. Kloster claimed to be a researcher in physics. Maybe it was true. Maybe he really had been at Heidelberg or Leipzig or who-knows-where. However, his focus had shifted and he was all caught up with issues that appeared strange and obscure to Umber. What was the connection between God and light? Was it possible to artificially reach a speed greater than light that does not exist in nature? Was it possible to come up with a mathematical formula for the speed of thought? What was the connection between light and fire? At least this much was clear to Umber who, though he lacked a scientific background, was not short on scientific method: Kloster reasoned more like a Zoroastrian sorcerer, or an Indian shaman than like a researcher at a university – and a German one at that!

This helped Umber overcome all his inhibitions, shed his academic garments that were never a perfect fit anyway, and confess his greatest desire and obsession. When

Kloster first heard him speak of the characters of future novels and his desire to get to know them, his whole face lit up. You could tell he was about to say something, but then held back. He was so lost in thought, as if some idea were throbbing in his brain, that he hardly spoke for the rest of the day. However, as soon as he saw Umber the next day, Kloster put his opened newspaper down on the bench, turned to him with a certain solemnity which Umber took to be a fusion of German seriousness and Iranian pride, and said solemnly: "I can help you get to know them."

"What?" replied Umber.

"You didn't understand?"

"No, sorry," replied Umber. He sat next to him while extracting a muffin from its little bag and beginning to pick at it.

"I see you're hungry."

"You're an ascetic, in my opinion. You are content with coffee and water that are more or less the same thing here."

"I am offering to help you realize your desire and you are talking to me about this nonsense?"

"I still don't understand."

"Listen, then. You told me that your obsessions are the characters from novels of the future that you will not be able to know, correct?"

"Of course. I ought to be ashamed, but that's how it is."

"So, I tell you again, I can help you get to know them."

Kloster grabbed Umber by the arm and held him

close. He looked him straight in the eyes. He had the blackest pupils and irises of the same indefinable color as his teeth. They looked like the eyes of someone who is raving from fever.

"You can?" asked Umber.

"Yes."

"But how? How is this possible?"

"By opening the door of time," answered Kloster. He almost winced yet maintained a calm and resolute expression.

Umber began to laugh, and then said: "The door of time? What's it like? Glass, hardwood, a folding door…?"

Kloster shook his head and took from the pocket of his corduroy jacket a small hexagonal mirror, not much bigger than a lady's compact, positioned it in such a way as to reflect the sun's rays, strong that morning, and he guided them toward a piece of newspaper that had fallen at his feet. With a sudden crackling, the piece of paper caught fire, burnt, and turned to ash. This made Umber tremble, with pins and needles down his spine. He had stopped laughing. He regretted his earlier sarcasm, and, although confused, he listened to what Kloster was saying:

"Just as in space one can capture fire from the sun, so in time one can capture the future from the eternal cycle of things. Everything has been and everything returns. It is not a question of seeing the future; rather, it is one of travelling there."

***

It took a few days for Umber to return to that topic. He noticed Kloster was indifferent, disposed to remain in silence. Offended, maybe. Umber was sure he had upset him with the comments he'd made about the door. He considered them stupid, yet ultimately forgivable. He figured it would only be right for him to ask Kloster about it.

On a rather cold, windy morning, with the blue ocean tormented by long grey shadows from the clouds, with no one on the benches near them and with the comforting warmth of that soupy coffee in paper cups, he asked: "You say there is a way to travel to the future?"

"There is."

"Space ships, flights to the galaxies…?"

"Nothing like that at all."

"But that's absurd. When you think about it, it's absurd…"

"If you're interested in future novels, we must travel to the libraries of the future."

"How the hell is that possible? How do you expect –?"

"We must open the door of a library of today that gives onto those to come," Kloster said, interrupting.

"But what does that mean?"

"Exactly what I said."

"How… how can you…?"

"That's my task. Trust me."

"Let's say I do trust you."

"That's important."

"And then?"

"After having opened the door, we must travel."

"*We* must?" asked Umber. "You too?"

"I'll prepare your voyage, if you decide to undertake it, and I'll come with you, just to help you. You know, I'm not particularly interested in novels, and I immediately forget those characters you're so obsessed with. I love music much more."

"So aren't you interested in the music of the future?"

"The best music is the one that flows... Listen to me... it's the music of what is happening now, as they used to say in Ireland, where they really understand music."

"But the characters in novels..."

"Libraries are full of them now, and they'll be full of them in the future. Don't ask me how, but they will be."

"Will we get to know books from the future?" asked Umber.

"We'll try."

"What will we need?"

"We need a library, four mirrors, and a beautiful sunset."

"That's it?" asked Umber as he began to laugh. He wasn't sure if it was from joy or contempt: toward himself and his desire to believe in his new friend.

***

Umber chose the library of the college where he was teaching. It was a large hall with big windows facing west where, when the curtains were opened, the rays of the setting sun would certainly have passed. He had to obtain permission to remain after hours. The librarian, who liked him because he was Italian – this sort of strange thing does occur when one travels and forgets one's nationality, left him the keys with a smirk that sealed a pact between them. Professor Umber would have access to the library after normal hours, from six pm onwards, that is. Having accepted the responsibility to securely close the main door and deposit the keys in the custodian's mailbox, he could remain all night to work as he pleased. The librarian certainly had no idea what kind of work was being done there. This thought caused a certain sick, villainous pleasure in Umber. He felt like Doctor Jekyll during teaching hours and like Mr. Hyde at sunset.

The evening when he and Kloster planned to meet in the library had arrived. Umber waited for the students to leave. In fact, they left in dribs and drabs just before six pm, all except for one who stayed behind with his elbows on the table and a notebook in front of him. Umber became impatient. He looked at that student of his – it had to be one of his students; the best one in the class who asked the most intelligent questions – with a kind of hatred. Why was he lingering over that book of criticism? Maybe it was René Wellek, possibly Erich

Auerbach, or even Harold Bloom. What was he searching for? What notes was he taking? Could he just be dilly-dallying because he guessed what was going to happen between these four walls? At that moment, Umber could have killed him. Fortunately, the student got up shortly after, passed in front of Umber to obsequiously say goodbye, and left.

At the library door, Umber made the agreed upon signal to Kloster with his arm. Kloster stealthily entered the room and right away looked around to see where the last rays of the sun would hit. This had to be fast. He found it quickly: It was on a bookshelf, the third level from the bottom. Without looking at the titles, he removed the volumes that occupied that spot and stacked them on a table. From the bag he had brought, he took out four hexagonal mirrors, larger than the ones he had used to ignite that piece of newspaper, and he put them against the wall to cover the open space. Umber followed his movements disconcertedly. Kloster moved with purpose yet calmly. He seemed to know what he was doing even if anyone else would have considered it absurd.

When the flame-red sun set on the horizon, its rays shone through the window whose curtains Umber had abruptly pulled aside and struck the mirrors laid out between the volumes. The calculation had turned out to be exact. A series of purple and golden rays radiated from that point, broke up, and fragmented into swirling vortexes. Kloster and Umber tried in vain to keep looking at the blinding, kaleidoscopic, flashing sparkle that radiated from the bookshelf all around them. A flame-shrouded cloud filled the room. In silence, Umber put one hand across his eyes.

Kloster seemed to be in a trance, almost inaudibly murmuring a mantra in the tongue of some ancient civilization. Then the sun went further down and the reflections faded, like sabers back in their dark sheaths, and yielded a still, weary, bluish light in the library. Umber moved and was about to turn on the neon ceiling lights. Kloster stopped him. He pointed to a table lamp in the distance and told him that would do. Umber went to it and turned on the switch; a dim light extended over the surface of the table. If someone from campus would have passed, he might have thought that Professor Umber was scrupulously planning his next lesson. Instead, he was listening to the ravings of Kloster who didn't even have the proper academic qualifications to be there.

"Now, we'll open the door," said Kloster.

"The door of the library?" asked Umber who was truly disoriented, almost frightened.

"No, come on…"

Kloster approached the bookshelf where the four mirrors had replaced the books. Umber followed him. At this point, something happened that Umber could never have imagined. Kloster moved one of the four mirrors from the wall as if it were a loose brick. But, instead of a wall, instead of something that any reason, logic, or experience would have revealed with mathematical precision, there appeared a vast blue hexagonal light like a screen, an opening toward something immaterial and distant that Umber, after a slight hesitation, trembling, and with his heart in his throat, finally dared to look at. So that was it – the door through time that Kloster had spoken of and to which he had initially referred with such irony? Did there exist a passage in space that overcame the limits of the material world?

Until that moment, Umber had been a modest disciple of Descartes and had believed in the division between *res cogitans* and *res extensa*. Yet, in front of what he was witnessing now, how could he orient himself? To which new system of thought should he turn? The hexagonal opening shrunk and expanded, and recognizable forms began to appear: a city square, tree-lined boulevards, traffic – but with unusual and different cars from the ones seen today, the comings-and-goings of a multicolored and teeming crowd of people, and then a building of glass, wood and steel. That's where the stunned glance of Umber and the tense one of Kloster were drawn. As soon as they entered, they recognized it as a library but they did not know from which city; it could have been Los Angeles or Atlanta, Brussels or Paris, Athens or Alexandria. Perhaps due to having spent too much time on some detail or other, they both thought it could have been the Bibliothèque Nationale, the one with four towers that looks like an open book that Mitterrand had wanted in Paris. Or the one inaugurated just a few years ago in Alexandria where the greatest, most famous library of antiquity had once stood. But they weren't sure.

The inside was spacious yet labyrinthine. There were many empty tables and computers turned off. It must have been night. Then they noticed one of the computers was still on. A calendar in the right corner of the screen indicated the date, 3-21-20 N.E, with 2109 in parentheses, evidently referring to the Christian era. In the middle of the screen there was a mythological figure, similar to a centaur, and beneath it a notice announcing the novels that had recently been acquired by the library.

Umber and Kloster never had the time to ask themselves if these novels existed in paper form or were to be read on the computer screen. They felt themselves being sucked into that library of the future, and suddenly they were there, in the flesh. It was as if they had passed through that opening and had travelled at a speed unknown until 2109 – or the year 20 of whatever New Era it was. It was Kloster who had the courage to click on that centaur-like creature and the first book cover appeared. It depicted a half-clad woman on the ground, surrounded by flames and men who looked like persecutors. The title was: *The Last Christian*. A brief description followed. Neither of them took notice of the author's name. Umber read with alarming pleasure and then grew melancholic as would often happen with the unexpected realization of a dream:

***

"Giustina France, orphaned at a very young age, has been tricked into practicing prostitution for the enjoyment of all those wealthy men who arrive in this city for tourism or on business. Giustina is tall, thin, with a well-sculpted face. Men like her for that intense look and the shameless sensuality with which she throws herself into the game. But Giustina harbors other feelings deep inside herself. That look of hers is not intense, except for the disgust she feels toward herself and others; that shameless sensuality is hopeless desperation. One day she decides to escape from that occupation and that city.

"Heeding her request for help, she brings with her a child, Gloria, who was sold by her family and forced into prostitution despite being a mere twelve. Their escape is arduous; a thousand dangers lay in store for them. Alienated, deceived, and betrayed by many, the two women avoid every beaten path. Giustina notices a new kind of courage growing inside her.

"While travelling further and further away from cities and villages, she comes upon an old, decrepit two-story building, abandoned among the debris, broken concrete and underbrush. She cannot believe anyone lives there. She enters with Gloria and finds a few old men and women who are terrorized by her arrival. They had hidden there to escape the sanctioned persecution of the last few Christians in that part of the planet. Once the terror has abated, Giustina France is greeted with generosity and kindness, especially by a woman called Sister Angela, and decides to stay with them. She places a cross around her neck, and dedicates herself to a life of prayer.

"Her companions are old, live in hiding, and know they could put up no resistance if they were discovered by the police and attacked. After a year, Gloria can no longer tolerate that environment of prayer and fear and decides to leave. She sneaks out one night. Now, everyone feels at risk because Gloria could be intercepted, sell them out, reveal their hideout. Giustina would like to leave again to seek out a more secure refuge. But the others do not have the strength to follow her. So she too stays, taking care of their illnesses, seeing to all their needs.

"Slowly, her companions die off, entrusting their souls to the God of whom they are the only believers in that part of the world. When Sister Angela also dies in her arms, Giustina remains alone in that hideout. Years pass, and then Gloria returns. Yet again, she has tired of the world that surrounds her. Giustina is happy to see her once more.

"However, unknown to Gloria, someone followed her. Someone saw the two women embrace, noticed the glimmer of a cross around the neck of one of them, and then, right after, the sign of the cross that the other one made before entering the old building in ruins. The police arrive and so do the bulldozers. The underbrush is set alight, the smoke spreads, Gloria runs out coughing and is struck by machine gun fire. Giustina remains in the old building, in front of a wooden cross that is burning, in the middle of the flames that spread everywhere. She too, the last Christian, will be burned at the stake."

***

Professor Umberto Umber was moved and seized by an uncontrollable agitation. He, the modest academic, the last wheel on the academic cart, was now able to speak about a character from a novel that would be written in one hundred years. Above all else, he was able to think of Giustina France as one of his conquests, tell stories about her, about her double life as a prostitute and martyr, think about how he would have helped her avoid the stake. He certainly would have helped her, but how?

He wanted to hug Kloster for having achieved their goal. However, the dignified and reserved attitude of his companion held him back. Now, Kloster seemed tired. Umber feared seeing him suddenly go and get the pile of books he had stacked on the table and put them back on the shelf, thus closing that miraculous window. But Kloster did not do that. Evidently, he wasn't tired, just focused and absorbed in his task. The one that hadn't yet been completed. Through that window into the future, the voyage could continue – he didn't know for how long, but he felt that it could. Umber begged him to do so. To go forward another century, at least.

Kloster moved another mirror. The hexagonal tunnel became longer. Although they hadn't moved, it was as if those two men were being sucked into that tunnel with even greater speed. They found themselves in a new library; the interior was different, so were the computer screens – they were bigger, double-sided, suspended on thin beams, and the image was perfect. The procedure, however, was still the same. Kloster clicked until he managed to see the cover and then the synopsis of a novel that had been acquired by the library in the last few months. The calendar read 3-21-120 N.E. The novel was written in a language unknown to either Umber or Kloster but they understood it was Anglo-Mandarin, a new language that was evidently very widespread on the planet at the time. Fortunately, the current language hadn't completely supplanted the others, much like the way the Euro had coexisted for a long time – at least with regards to pricing – with the Lira or French Franc, thought Umber. So, Kloster activated the convertor and the process worked. The text appeared in English. Umber began reading with hurried attention. *John Wei, Police Commissioner* was summarized thusly:

***

"John Wei had been a hero in the war that lasted for years and years. He had taken part in a campaign in Pakistan as a driver of tanks like the Dragonfly ESS101 that could transform themselves into helicopters and amphibious vehicles. He had led a successful attack and once, when his tank was destroyed, he continued to fight as an infantryman armed only with a large knife and hand grenades. It has been said that he killed fifty-six enemies singlehandedly.

"Recalled home after having been wounded and spending entire weeks on the verge of death, the still young John Wei – who recovered with surprising vigor – was named Police Commissioner of his city, a megalopolis of 59 million inhabitants. This is how the authorities thought to compensate him for his wartime heroism. However, John Wei, who had stared death in the face, was tired of killing and scared of dying himself. When a cargo ship with all its goods exploded in his city's port – an endless 150 km of quays – and claimed sailors among the victims, it was up to John Wei to coordinate the investigations.

"The Police Commissioner understood right away that the power to undertake an attack of those dimensions could only have been mustered by the Order of the White Dragon, a criminal organization that wanted to take over the port and manage all its traffic. Unsuccessful in their takeover, the bosses of the Order of the White Dragon had planned that bloody attack as a warning. Then they carried on. After another cargo ship blew up, they raised the stakes: A moored navy frigate was blown up there with fifteen servicemen and three officers on board. The fear was that the next target would be a passenger liner, one of those new cruise ships capable of transporting thirty thousand people across the oceans.

"John Wei had to avoid that. That was his job as Police Commissioner. In the meantime, another matter from another aspect of his life disturbed his sleep. He had fallen in love with one of his staff, a blonde and attractive police official, Jasmine Gard. He couldn't resist her but he knew that the law would prohibit his marrying her precisely because she was a member of his staff, and he feared that at the slightest declaration of love she could have dragged him in shame to the STSRC, the Special Tribunal for Sexual and Romantic Conduct. Therefore, he kept this passion of his to himself.

"He takes charge of all the inquiries and the war against the Order of the White Dragon with gloomy, intense energy. Having to select an agent to infiltrate the Order, he chooses Jasmine Gard. Not even he knows for sure whether it is to distance her from him in order to forget her – with the risk of having her die – or to offer her a grand and unique opportunity for career advancement. The operation fails; Jasmine Gard is discovered, tortured, and killed.

"More alone than ever before, in despair, and full of self-loathing, John Wei renews his efforts. It is as if he must avenge himself. It is like a new war, more terrible than the one he fought when he was young. The port continues to be the scene of repeated bloodbaths. Police Commissioner John Wei discovers that among the city officials there are informers for the Order of the White Dragon. He drives out the corrupt officials, but he slowly discovers new plots of collusion between the people in power and the criminal organizations. He will never be able to stop them completely, and he knows it. Then, obsessed by thoughts of Jasmine Gard, he kills himself with a shot to the temple while sitting at his desk."

***

Kloster looked at his watch. He wasn't sure how much more time they still had. He firmly moved the third of the four mirrors he had put on the bookshelf. The men glided silently and very quickly through the tunnel and found themselves in a library in the year 220 N.E. which, according to a rapid calculation, should have corresponded to 2309 A.D. Umber was overexcited, almost trembling, and asked if he could further impose on Kloster to read the synopses of more novels. The place they were in now looked nothing like what had traditionally been regarded as a library. There were no tables, chairs, or keyboards – just very long lines of flat screens fitted against the walls. While standing, you pressed the screen with a finger and vivid, swirling, abstract colors would be emitted, as well as oral instructions on how to proceed.

Initially, the language that the metallic, yet sweet voice used was incomprehensible to Umber and Kloster. These two men made many attempts, pressing their index fingers against so many icons. Finally, some written instructions appeared in a language very similar to German. The words were backlit and the vocal instructions were also in that form of German contaminated by French and other Nordic languages, possibly Swedish or Icelandic. It was much tougher to understand the spoken version than the written one. Kloster carried on. The list of the library's latest acquisitions was long. He chose one at random. The cover that appeared was of *Chimera I Ruled Over Us*:

***

"After an error in a secret eugenics lab of a multinational corporation with headquarters in Hamburg, a population of half-human and half-animal creatures emerged and began to spread out. This population was completely beyond the control of humans (in the strict sense of the word) who, for a very brief period at the beginning, were seen as fathers or progenitors but, soon after, were considered enemies to be chased out and destroyed. Among the many species created – butterfly-men, mouse-men, snake-men, swallow-men, dolphin men (whose females were perfect reproductions of the ancient sirens), horse-men (similar to the centaurs of old), the eagle-men and squid-men were the strongest and most intelligent.

"The former, capable of flight and with fierce beaks, lived in the fields and woods; the latter, who took control of the coastline, were amphibious (men from the waist up but with six tentacles instead of legs), and extremely fast with frightful prehensile strength. Then, they advanced on the cities, attacking from on high, installing themselves on roofs, and pouring in from rivers, canals, and every waterway.

"Chimera (his laboratory number was H6112MT) established himself as leader, the one who knew how to keep the armies of eagle-men and squid-men united and focused. When they ceased their geographical expansion and found themselves in control of a territory that included parts of Germany, Holland, Belgium, France, Switzerland, and Italy, Chimera was elected king and became Chimera I. The new capital was built on the Rhine, a city of canals (in which the squid- men navigated) and of high towers with broad roofs where the eaglemen lived, ready to take flight.

"Basic humans had lost everything and lived as poor slaves. Despite his warrior instinct, Chimera I was not cruel. He looked like a squid-man but had the brain and eyes of an eagle. Very few human weaknesses still existed in him. He had no emotions; he felt neither desire nor mercy. Reluctant to start a family, he adopted a child of the eagle-men and appointed him as his heir. He was to be Chimera II and would keep the kingdom united. On the distant borders, Chimera I did not start wars, nor could he be provoked into one.

"However, he knew that sooner or later he would be attacked, that the great human powers of the planet would not tolerate his sovereignty over a large part of Europe and that his troops would struggle to beat back the attacks. Internally, he found himself having to quell insurrections. They were caused by the humans within the borders of his empire who did not accept their state of slavery. Amongst themselves, they muttered words that Chimera I had prohibited – democracy, liberty, republic – and they took on the task of toppling him. It was like a dream yet he felt that, despite his commitment as sovereign and the strength of the squid-men and eagle-men, the dream would soon end."

***

The obsession to know more characters grew stronger and Professor Umber asked Kloster, while almost grabbing his wrist, to press his index finger on the screen again, even at random. Another book cover appeared. There was a title in tiny characters, *R66Dklein*, and a promotional blurb in enormous letters: *THE FIRST NOVEL WRITTEN BY A ROBOT*. It was still in that hybrid German language that Kloster was nonetheless able to read and translate for Umber:

***

"R66Dklein is a rather small robot, the size of a child, basically, who recounts the story of his being in the service of humans, the events of his day, and his participation in the life of his master and family. R66Dklein describes his days with neutral precision – the time he begins his work, the time he prepares breakfast, the time he walks Wolfgang, the family dog. Though he doesn't much care for the cat, Mozart, he doesn't possess the correct expressions to explain this. He writes with an apparently pre-programmed linguistic ability that leaves no room for expressions of doubt, fear or anxiety.

"Here are some of his first lines, before his language became more fluid: 'Time 6:05, awake. Check my battery status, superior motor functions – Time 6:15, open windows, check weather conditions nice sun – Time 6:35, exercise to improve my fitness, my fitness important – Time 7:15, enter kitchen to prepare breakfast for masters – Time 7:18, coffee in cups, toast with butter, fresh cheese, fruit, everything ready – Time 7:19, Thor enters barefoot yells at little brother Werner asks for extra slice of bread puts fingers in cheese – Time 7:25, damn Mozart enters kitchen.'

"Even if he narrates funny details, you know that he laughs at them only with his human masters' permission. Even if he appears rather inclined toward mirth, it doesn't fall within the range of his options and reactions. And yet, the description of his masters' children, Thor and Werner (children as tall as he is, his playmates), has something fresh about it and one notices an approximate likeness to human nature.

"R66Dklein plays because he is programmed to play. He imitates Thor and Werner yet occasionally he manages to feel superior to them in terms of fitness, consistency, and energy. When his master is called up as an Officer for the Great Human War against a dark kingdom populated by monstrous creatures, R66Dklein follows him as his squire. His departure and goodbyes to Thor and Werner ('Bye Thor Bye Werner I'm going going going going away away away away away Oh I'm going I won't see you I'm going Oh no I'm going away going away Oh no no') has moments of peculiar warmth, if not real emotion. His loyalty to his master during various occasions in the war shows some generosity that would be incorrect to refer to as a sense of devotion or friendship, but does resemble it.

"R66Dklein narrates the tale with his artificial intelligence. However, what is striking is that in his narration there seems to be developing, albeit slowly, the beginnings of a soul. He displays jealousy toward another robot-squire of an officer-friend of his master; he misses the comforts of home; he is horrified by the monstrous creatures the humans engage in battle. He never arrives at introspection or displays a sense of self, but you notice that he is almost there. He doesn't manage to laugh or cry with that titanium and crystal face of his but you notice that, at least in his writing, he would like to. The story ends with his return home, his embraces of Thor and Werner, his first quarrel with Mozart, the cat, and his lunch of chocolate-flavored lubricating oil."

***

Kloster made a signal to Umber that they had to hurry and pressed his index finger on the screen in order to display another book cover. The title of the new novel appeared in an Arabic script that Umber could not read. Kloster, who had learned Farsi from his mother Jamilé, managed rather well and with a different voice – warmer, almost inspired – he translated the synopsis of the novel for Umber. It was titled, *Saida is in Love*:

***

"Saida, a woman of striking beauty, was young when the Islamic partisan groups engaged those of the CACU (Chinese-American Commercial Union) in Pakistan and Afghanistan, and the Christian armies kept them busy in Africa and South America. Of unshakeable Islamic faith – with her head always swathed in an emerald-green veil, Saida displayed such courage and energy that her fame grew among all soldiers, even the enemy. There was so much talk about her that she even became the inspiration of legends and songs. If for the rebels (and even the Christians) she was as unrelenting as the sea and as beautiful as a rose, for her enemies she was a hag and a whore on whose head there was a bounty of a million Hong Kong Yuan-dollars. You couldn't count the number of ESS 201 Winged Dragon tanks that she'd blown up, or the close-quarter combats she'd won against the better-trained and better-armed soldiers of the Sino-American army.

"Saida was a Fury, and everyone worshipped, feared, or despised her but no one loved her. She realized this after she victoriously led the rebels into a city that until then had been held by the enemy who, worn out by the immense destruction, finally surrendered. Those were dark days, full of vendettas, abuses of power, and horror. In the rest of the world, the struggle continued. It was clear that the rebels would carry on with every means and at any cost – even the total destruction of civilization – as long as it meant the demise of the CACU and its power.

"Saida wanted nothing more to do with it. She had laid down her arms. She was still very beautiful and she finally realized it. Her skin was brown like chestnut honey; her hair was black; her eyes were long and the color of jade; her body was firm yet supple where it was supposed to be. Although famous throughout the world, she fell in love with an unknown, simple, young man with soft features who earned his living by telling ancient fables and love stories. She discovered that she would have to face the disapproval of her fellow soldiers and friends who called her back to her warrior duties. She did this with the same energy as before. She battled against everyone. She, who had inspired tales of bloodshed, now wanted to live a life listening to tales of love from the lips of the young man she was to marry."

***

Kloster stopped and looked again at his watch. Umber was in a state of ecstasy due to that rich bounty of characters of the future that he now knew: Giustina France, John Wei, Chimera I, R66Dklein, and Saida. There was one more mirror to move. Kloster did not know how long that door of the tunnel to the future would remain open. The night was slipping away, the deciphering of difficult, corrupted languages (Franco-German-Swedish, the tongue of the Chimera-men, that constricted idiom of the first autobiographical novel written by a robot, the Arabic with Farsi, Turkish, and Urdu influences that related the story of Saida) had consumed Kloster who every once in a while needed to catch his breath and take a sip of water. This had to be fast. Umber was impatient, pressing right up against Kloster.

"Just one more, I beg you!" Umber muttered to Kloster.

"It's the last one."

"I realize it."

So, Kloster moved the last mirror. The hexagonal tunnel became even larger but the light that passed through it seemed to dim quickly. There were no more library walls. There were no computers, no screens. All you heard was the crash of the surf. There were expanses of sound and waves. They listened to the wind whistle in their ears and felt the sand in their eyes. The seagulls and crows cawed as they soared on high, above the palm trees. Then, in the moonlight, there appeared a path that led from the beach to a very green hill. Passing gigantic trees – oaks, pines, and eucalyptus – they arrived at a stone hut, as tall as a tower, with narrow windows that looked more like slits. A dim light emanated from those windows and smoke issued from the chimney.

They entered slowly, carefully placing each step. In the half-light, they noticed a fireplace with little flames. They saw a bookshelf with rolls of a paper-like material, then a table. On the table there was a sheet with a date written on it: V AE 2409 after Christ, year 1777 of Egira. And some words in Latin: "Today, I, brother (followed by some illegible letters) discovered a short story written in a language of long and illustrious history that is no longer spoken, derived from Latin. In this story, we find the following strange events, that I have summarized here."

Umber and Kloster read in unison. They would never have thought to end up with Latin, a language they both translated with ease. What's more, it appeared to be an easy Latin, heavily influenced by subsequent, barbarian languages. Vernal Equinox, 21 March, four centuries ago. They carried on, and the first surprise for Professor Umber – the Italian without a homeland who had tumbled down to California (that no-man's land) – was that he was confronted with his own language:

"Along the sea, not far from here, there met two solitary men of the same age who were possessed by the same absurd passions. They became friends or, at least, they developed a kind of routine whereby they could be seen every morning walking and talking about their plans and dreams. They were no longer young and it seemed that they had not been able to forge ties to anything solid and real in the world. In any case, it was a time when there was nothing solid or real in the world. They lived on dreams.

"These learned men had devoted themselves to the pursuit of their desires – their unbridled passions – and all their years of experience hadn't helped them mend their ways. On the contrary, the thought of the brief time left to them had pushed them further to follow their illusions. One of them had the audacity to challenge the laws of Light and God; the other, more frivolous one had joined the first in that challenge to satisfy a mad desire to get to know the characters from future novels. One day, the former proposed to the latter to open the door of time, to join in a mad journey to future centuries, and the latter unfortunately accepted..."

***

Umber and Kloster, overcome by a wave of terror, did not need to proceed any further – they would have found their own names, their twilight rendezvous in the library, the four magic mirrors on the bookshelf against the wall that were moved like wobbly bricks – to understand beyond the shadow of a doubt, with a trembling deep in the pits of their stomachs, and a distressing giddiness that that short story was about them and that they were its characters. And, what made their blood run even colder was that it was about to reveal the destiny awaiting them. What would have happened to them there, in that darkness of 2409 – an immense, post-apocalyptic darkness barely disturbed by the flickering fire? Would they have managed to find their way home?

Another wave of terror cascaded over them. They could read no further nor would they have wanted to. From the fear and cold that suddenly assailed him, Professor Umber's teeth began to chatter uncontrollably. Kloster coughed and gulped down the rest of the water in the bottle. Both of them backed up with eyes closed. Then Kloster retraced the steps between him and the volumes he had removed from the bookshelf, moving with the geometrical precision of an astronaut in space. Once those books were in his hands, he put them back in their place. The wall re-emerged with its opacity and consistency intact. The stiff edges of the book covers produced a dull thud when they were back in the shelf. Kloster checked that those four hexagonal mirrors were again in his bag. Rather than sling it over his shoulder, he put it under his arm. At that moment, the stream of whitish light from the approaching dawn crept through the windows and into the room. There, the darkness slowly faded. They exited, running like thieves.

Umber, whose teeth continued to chatter, was about to forget to leave the keys to the library in the custodian's letterbox. He remembered as he was sitting behind the wheel of his car. He didn't understand why, but he only began to feel more secure once he had returned and turned on the ignition. They headed for the boardwalk of Laguna Beach. There was no traffic at all. They arrived in moments. They did not exchange a single word. They were afraid of their own individual silences and the one between them. They were not sure that they had returned to their own time. Maybe the two old hippies and devoted dreamers who had stumbled into California had ripped themselves out of it and would never find it again. That asphalt road, the four lanes, the traffic lights – yes; those buildings, villas – yes; but the waves of the ocean, the sand of the beach, the color of the sky, were they still the same as the ones they would have seen if they had awaited the dawn in that distant future?

What would have happened to them if they had stayed? And how did that monk-scribe who had possibly been sleeping in the next room get their story? Who had written it? They were going over the characters they had met and their stories in their minds. Persecutions, mafias, disasters, monstrous beings, wars. But also devotion, passion, heroism, play, love. Like yesterday, like always.

***

They began to feel better when the first vendor opened his stand and they bought brimming cups of coffee. With trembling hands that struggled to pull out a bill from his wallet, Umber bought a muffin too. Only one because he knew Kloster would not have eaten any, not even on that day. They strolled along the sand, drinking and warming themselves up. The sun rose from the horizon, increasing in strength and color, to become an immense, red flame reflected on the rippling ocean.

Finally, someone came by. Two homeless people who dropped a mountain of ripped black bags of who-knows-what and laid themselves out on the grass of the gardens with their dirty, heavy beards turned toward the sunlight as if to wash them. Then, the old lady in the white track suit arrived and she sat in the lotus position to meditate, and recite yoga mantras and Zen prayers. Then, two girls in low-rise jeans, tight, short tops, and sparkling piercings in their navels walked together in an embrace along the beach. Soon, Diane Keaton would pass by with her cool grace — you could count on it.

"Do you know what I'm thinking?" asked Umber whose teeth had finally stopped chattering so that he could at last take a bite of his muffin.

"No," replied Kloster, slurping his coffee from its big white paper cup with a straw.

"The present is beautiful," said Umber, his mouth full.

"Really?" said Kloster with a smile.

Laguna Beach – Sanremo, February/March 2009

I PERSONAGGI DEI ROMANZI FUTURI

Dovuto a Mark Axelrod

Da qualche parte, nella sua giovinezza moderatamente hippie, Umberto Umber aveva letto che la California è al fondo di un piano inclinato, e che tutto quello che non ha radici vi rotola. Arrivato a una età più che matura, e sentendosi sempre e totalmente privo di attaccamento a qualunque cosa, piuttosto che rotolarvi aveva preferito scivolare tranquillamente in California con un incarico in una Università e prendendo casa a Laguna Beach, dove, a distanza di migliaia e migliaia di chilometri, sembra di essere in una Costa Azzurra più estesa e più tranquilla. Il Professor Umber non aveva legami con niente di reale. Era italiano anche se in Italia il nome lo faceva scambiare spesso per straniero, e, in patria e all'estero, non c'era collega che non scherzasse con lui sulla strana assonanza tra il suo nome e quello del protagonista di un celeberrimo romanzo del XX secolo. Lui sorrideva paziente osservando che gli sarebbero occorse due acca e una ti in più per essere davvero omonimo del personaggio di *Lolita*, e aggiungeva con un'occhiata maliziosa che per di più le ninfette non gli erano mai piaciute. Ed era vero. Nessuna sua allieva lo aveva mai tentato. Non aveva mai avuto amanti. Era stato sposato con una donna energica e volitiva, un' avvocato che guadagnava dieci volte più di lui. Il matrimonio era finito dopo qualche anno, così dolcemente che non si ricordava neppure più il perché. Pensava di essere stato fortunato, sapeva bene, dai casi di tanti colleghi, a quali rovine psichiche e finanziarie un divorzio può condurre. Non aveva nessuna proprietà. I genitori, che aveva perduto presto, gli avevano lasciato un appartamento e qualche pacchetto di azioni. Lui aveva venduto tutto.

Dopo il divorzio, aveva affittato sempre appartamenti ammobiliati, riducendo all'osso gli oggetti da trasportare a ogni trasloco. Gli bastavano due vani, se erano su un porto ancora meglio. Era professore di letteratura comparata, i libri che gli servivano per il suo lavoro li trovava nelle biblioteche delle diverse Università che lo incaricavano di tenere corsi. Così Umberto Umber si spostava leggero come una piuma. Anche il suo guardaroba era essenziale. Poche giacche, tante T-shirt e camicie, jeans, mocassini. In California gli bastava quello. Stava a Laguna Beach, in collina, su quella collina che gli incendi periodicamente devastano, ma a una distanza ragionevole, che poteva coprire comodamente con una passeggiata, dalla spiaggia di sabbia fine e color avorio di fronte all'Oceano aperto.

Aveva conservato abitudini europee, al mattino scendeva a fare colazione in un caffè, beveva cappuccino con un muffin o un croissant e intanto sfogliava il *Los Angeles*

Times in cerca di notizie curiose. La sera cenava spesso in un ristorante dove oramai i camerieri lo conoscevano e lo salutavano con una stretta di mano cordiale quando entrava e quando usciva, dopo aver mangiato qualche copiosa insalata di gamberi o di tacchino accompagnata da un bicchiere di vino rosso. Era un uomo la cui vita non stava a cuore a nessuno. Non c'era una donna che lo amasse, né lui sentiva il bisogno che ci fosse. Aveva allievi e allieve, ma era evidente che chiunque di loro, per proseguire il corso dei propri studi, poteva fare a meno di lui. Aveva molte conoscenze, ma nessun vero amico.

Del resto, non avrebbe saputo cosa condividere con un amico, non avrebbe saputo neppure di cosa parlare, perché non gli interessava niente, la vita universitaria, la politica, lo sport, l'economia non avevano ai suoi occhi nessun fascino. Non si lasciava neppure sopraffare dai ricordi, nonostante l'età fosse ormai avanzata. Nessuna nostalgia lo legava all'Italia, dove era nato e cresciuto, alla Francia, dove aveva insegnato diversi anni, alla sua giovinezza. Scivolare in California era stato naturale per lui, nessun appiglio lo tratteneva. E ora si era fermato di fronte alla vastità incommensurabile del Pacifico. Verso sera usciva di nuovo e se ne stava a lungo sulla passeggiata a mare, tra i giardini, le passerelle in legno, le panchine, poi scendeva sulla sabbia, guardava l'orizzonte. Al di là dell'orizzonte, c'era l'Asia, il Sol Levante. Lui stava bene lì, nella luce del tramonto.

Se è vero che il Professor Umberto Umber non aveva legami con niente di reale, questo non vuol dire che non avesse legami in assoluto. Ne aveva eccome. Ma con esseri la cui vita si manifesta soltanto nel mondo della immaginazione, esseri che sono le forme più vive e concrete della irrealtà. Ne aveva con i personaggi dei libri, poemi e romanzi, che man mano aveva letto nel corso della sua esistenza, e verso i quali aveva sviluppato un amore morboso, tutto fatto di fantasticherie e di finzioni ulteriori. Rimasto oscuro come studioso, aveva pubblicato il minimo per poter continuare una a sua volta oscura carriera accademica. Il fatto è che a un rapporto critico, di cui pure riconosceva la necessità e la grandezza in qualche modo eroica, preferiva senza esitazioni un rapporto amoroso, licenzioso, con i personaggi della letteratura. Era una debolezza, e lo sapeva. Forse una vergogna. Ma non poteva farci niente.

Come tantissimi adolescenti si era innamorato dei fantasmi di celluloide delle grandi dive di allora, soprattutto di Gina Lollobrigida e di Marilyn Monroe. Con la prima aveva immaginato brevi avventure consumate durante viaggi in Rolls Royce, baci caldissimi su labbra stupendamente disegnate e su un collo e un seno bianchi come la farina, la neve, lo zucchero. Quando poi, uomo fatto, aveva una volta incrociato la diva, ormai a sua volta donna anziana, in un aeroporto, era stata ancora la bianchezza assoluta della sua pelle ad impressionarlo. Con Marilyn, era stata un'altra cosa. Una vera e propria storia d'amore. Aveva ballato con lei meglio di Yves Montand in *Facciamo l'amore*, l'aveva baciata meglio di Tony Curtis in *A qualcuno piace caldo*, aveva conversato con lei meglio di Arthur Miller la sera che a un party le prese tra le dita un alluce e cominciò a sedurla. Ne era geloso. Sprofondava nella sua carnalità, ne riemergeva puro spirito. L'amava come se l'avesse avuta lì nella sua camera di ragazzo, tutta per sé. Quando gli giunse la notizia del suo suicidio, gli sembrò di aver perduto una parte del suo mondo, la più innocente e morbosa.

Ma in quello stesso periodo si manifestarono i primi segni di un innamoramento che, a differenza del primo, ben pochi avrebbero condiviso, per non dire nessuno. Il ragazzo Umber cominciò a isolare personaggi dalle pagine dei suoi primi libri, e cominciò a fantasticare su di essi, a sognarli, a condividere con essi ore e ore delle sue giornate. E poi aveva continuato così. Era il suo segreto, la sua malattia incurabile. Dall'*Odissea* gli era entrata nella fantasia la giovane principessa Nausicaa. Come se i versi di Omero non bastassero, nella sua follia Umber aggiungeva tocchi di colore al personaggio, immaginava pettinatura, andatura, abiti, e andava oltre, labbra, mani, seno, cosce, niente poneva un limite alla sua impudicizia e alla sua smania.

Dalla *Divina Commedia*, senza rispetto alcuno, aveva prelevato Francesca da Rimini, e, sostituendosi a Paolo, riviveva decine di volte l'adulterio con lei dopo che un libro d'amore aveva sospinto gli occhi dell'uno in quelli dell'altra facendoli impallidire, sudare, tremare a morte. Per anni era stato fidanzato con Rosalind, la protagonista di *As you like it*. A lui piaceva proprio così, una ragazza, come quella che Shakespeare aveva saputo immaginare vagabonda sotto mentite spoglie nella foresta di Arden, con una così naturale forza di attrazione che nessun travestimento poteva attutire. Poi, aveva amato perdutamente Ottilia, il personaggio delle *Affinità elettive*. Ne aveva condiviso i pensieri, i dolori, si continuava a commuovere sino alle lacrime di fronte alla chimica ineluttabilità del suo destino.

Non si era dato limiti, Umber. Tra Frollo e Quasimodo, Phoebus e Gringoire, si era lasciato sedurre da Esmeralda, la bella e fatale zingara di *Notre Dame de Paris*, aveva vagabondato nel verde dolce del Friuli e per le fondamenta di Venezia con la Pisana delle *Confessioni di un Italiano*, aveva rotto gli argini di ogni pudore con Connie Chatterley, era andato a colazione non soltanto da Tiffany, ma in tutte le migliori gioiellerie e i migliori ristoranti di New York, Parigi, Londra con Holly Golightly. Non bisogna credere però che questi amori avessero un'unica natura sessuale. Umber si innamorava della donna soltanto se era ai suoi occhi un personaggio letterario felicemente riuscito.

Con la maturità, si innamorò sovente anche di personaggi maschili. Il catalogo sarebbe troppo lungo, certo è che intrattenne rapporti con Robinson Crusoe, Tristram Shandy, Padre Cristoforo, David Copperfield, Jean Valjean, Achab, il Capitano Nemo, Jim Hawkins, Sherlock Holmes, Andrej Bolkonskij, Dick Diver, Leopold Bloom, Cosimo di Rondò e tanti tanti altri. Con un personaggio in testa, con cui dialogare, di cui immaginare nuove avventure, non era mai né solo né infelice. Erano questi i legami che davano un senso alla sua vita, che la riempivano, alle volte anche di una gioia debordante, assurda ma inalienabile, di cui quasi aveva pudore.

Potete ben immaginare lo sconforto che prendeva il Professor Umberto Umber quando udiva tanti suoi dotti colleghi, molto più quotati di lui in campo accademico, che discettavano sulla "morte del romanzo". Per lui, la morte del romanzo voleva dire la morte di una folla di personaggi con cui vivere in compagnia, la morte della più grande parte di se stesso. Ma per sua fortuna in California queste teorie erano attecchite di meno. E lui passeggiando sul mare di Laguna Beach poteva continuare a domandarsi come avrebbe potuto salvare Esmeralda dal pugnale turpe di Frollo, o a immaginare Connie Chatterley a cinquant'anni che tradiva Mellors con un giovane aristocratico, perché no?

***

Quando certe mattine Umberto Umber vedeva correre sul lungomare Diane Keaton, che abitava lì vicino, non era lei che inseguiva con lo sguardo, ma la musa di Woody Allen, la protagonista con Jack Nicholson di un film straordinariamente divertente e sexy sull'amore in età non più verde di cui non ricordava il titolo. Ancora una volta, era il personaggio ad avere la meglio sull'essere reale. Le attrici che preferiva, in questa sua tarda stagione, erano Angelina Jolie e Jennifer Lopez. La prima così filiforme, come snodabile, con quel suo volto algido, già post- umano, tutto risolto in labbra che sembravano di un materiale diverso della carne, gli appariva il modello delle donne del futuro. La seconda era il presente, era la dolcezza piena, rotonda, palpabile della vita che scorre ora, come un fiume tranquillo, sicuro tra le sue sponde, sicuro di arrivare al mare. Jennifer Lopez, se avesse potuto scegliere, avrebbe scelto la stella del firmamento latino, voce, colore, calore, culo, di lei tutto lo attirava, senza più provocargli, naturalmente, i turbamenti dell'adolescenza.

Quando Umber andava a bere un caffè all' 8600 di Sunset Boulevard, West Hollywood, gli piaceva poi passeggiare con il sole alle spalle sin dove il Sunset incrocia La Ciniega Boulevard, che scende a precipizio lunghissimo, rettilineo con soltanto qualche scarto geometrico, verso il mare. Gli sembrava di percorrere con lo sguardo non una strada, ma un canyon tagliato nel corpo vivente della città, e quando poi ripassava di lì che era ormai notte si incantava a veder La Ciniega boulevard percorso da una marea di lava in un senso e nell'altro da un luccicare continuo, densissimo, di polvere di stelle dorate. Arrivava sino alla sagoma turrita, neogotica e un po' assurda del Chateau Marmont, nelle cui camere avevano vissuto tante attrici e tanti attori che avevano imprestato la loro immagine ai personaggi che avevano fatto sognare le platee più vaste su tutto il pianeta, e Umber pensava a Clark Gable in *Via col vento*, a William Holden in *L'amore è una cosa meravigliosa*.

Ma, molto stranamente, i personaggi dei film lo toccavano meno di quelli dei romanzi, cui poteva dare il corpo e la voce che preferiva lui, contribuendo a ricrearli con la sua personale fantasia. Così, passeggiando lì, tra l'8600 e l'8200 di Sunset Boulevard, Umber pensava ad Angelina Jolie e a Jennifer Lopez, ma si rendeva conto subito che se invece di donne in carne (Jennifer) e ossa (Angelina) e star di Hollywood fossero state protagoniste di qualche romanzo, se le avesse scoperte tra le pagine di qualche libro, gli sarebbero piaciute molto, molto di più.

Era una malattia che Umber non sapeva come chiamare, sapeva di esserne affetto, e non solo non voleva guarirne, ma sentiva con un piacere sottile e malinconico che col passare degli anni peggiorava, che quella sua passione diventava una specie innocente di pazzia.

Da studioso, da lettore, Umber sapeva tutto su tanti personaggi di romanzi già scritti e pubblicati e inventariati nelle storie letterarie. Ma quella sua specie di pazzia lo portò a tormentarsi di non sapere niente di niente su quelli che sarebbero venuti, che si sarebbero aggiunti, che sarebbero stati al centro dei romanzi pronti ad occupare nuove vetrine delle librerie e nuovi scaffali nelle biblioteche del mondo. Man mano che il tempo passava, che gli acciacchi dell'età si sentivano – le notti che stentava ad addormentarsi, che scendeva da letto due o tre volte per andare in bagno ad orinare, le giornate che un dolore acuto al ginocchio destro gli impediva di passeggiare sulla spiaggia – il pensiero che non avrebbe conosciuto neppure uno dei personaggi dei romanzi futuri lo cominciò ad ossessionare. Accentuando le proprie precauzioni, tenendo sotto stretto controllo la pressione arteriosa e il livello del colesterolo, evitando il fumo, anche la pipa che gli era sempre così piaciuta, eliminando i grassi animali, limitando l'alcool a quel bicchiere di vino rosso serale, mentre un tempo si era lasciato andare non poco al whisky e al cognac, assumendo appropriati integratori, facendo quel po' di esercizio fisico che una pigrizia congenita e una artrosi acquisita gli consentivano, poteva presumere di vivere ancora una ventina d'anni. Una ventina d'anni nei quali sarebbe venuto a conoscenza di nuovi personaggi usciti dalla fantasia degli autori di romanzi, li avrebbe valutati, seguiti, interrogati, rivissuti.

E poi? Nella sua pazzia, inoffensiva ma non meno preoccupante, l'aspetto della morte che lo impensieriva e lo turbava di più era questo. Che non avrebbe più potuto sapere niente di quali nuove Emma Bovary e quali nuovi Papà Goriot, ma neppure di quali nuove Miss Marple e di quali nuovi Maigret sarebbero apparsi all'orizzonte. La cosa gli riusciva intollerabile. E ci pensava e ripensava, continuamente. Ma quale rimedio poteva mai trovare a qualcosa che si presentava con la ineluttabilità delle leggi della natura e del destino di noi mortali?

***

Non era certo all'immortalità personale che tendeva Umberto Umber. Gli bastava una conoscenza che andasse oltre i confini della sua esistenza, non era poco, lo riconosceva, ma non era neppure una pretesa che lo mettesse in concorrenza con Dio, immortale per definizione. Tutto quello che nasce, muore, si diceva Umber pensando con una buona rassegnazione alla propria condizione di nato da donna. Ma i personaggi dei romanzi, i grandi personaggi, nati da uomini e da donne anche loro, perché hanno varcato i secoli, i millenni, e noi possiamo ancora commuoverci, ridere, indignarci, naufragare, viaggiare, tremare, correre, amare con loro? C'è un mistero in questa sopravvivenza più che umana, una scintilla del divino che abita in essi, si diceva Umberto Umber, sempre più preso da questi pensieri.

Una mattina, sul lungomare di Laguna Beach, vide un tipo che era la prima volta che compariva lì. Su una panchina di fianco alla sua una signora dai capelli grigi, in una elegante tuta bianca, stava meditando in posizione del loto, su un'altra due giovinette, una in jeans e giubbotto neri, l'altra con gonne corte e camicetta variopinta, strette l'una all'altra parlavano ognuna per suo conto al rispettivo cellulare, tra molte risate tintinnanti. Nonostante ciò, il tipo seduto sulla panchina centrale non si voltava a guardarle, né infastidito né incuriosito. Era un uomo della età di Umber. Da come era vestito, giacca di velluto leggera e stazzonata, pantaloni di cotone, sandali ai piedi, e dal volto, occhiali dalla montatura di tartaruga, una barba grigia non troppo curata, si sarebbe detto un professore anche lui. Il colorito della pelle era piuttosto scuro, gli occhi neri e profondi, e insieme tradivano una origine asiatica. Poteva essere indiano, pakistano, iraniano, non era facile distinguerlo. Stava leggendo il *Los Angeles Times*, e intanto da un bicchiere di carta sorbiva lentamente un liquido che doveva essere caffè.

Senza una ragione, con quelle decisioni che nascono da un istinto più profondo dei sensi stessi, Umber si andò a sedere proprio su quella panchina, proprio vicino allo sconosciuto. Si mise a leggere anche lui il giornale, e se ne stettero così, paralleli l'uno all'altro, somiglianti più che il colore della pelle non dicesse, per quasi un'ora. Anche quella mattina passò Diane Keaton lì davanti, nessuno dei due ebbe un commento da fare.

***

L'indomani Umber trovò quel tipo sulla stessa panchina. Anche la signora che faceva meditazione yoga nella posizione del loto, per altro, era fedele alla sua lì di fianco. Si sedette. I due rimasero vicini a lungo, sempre senza parlarsi. Umber ebbe il sospetto che non conoscesse l'inglese. Poi ricordò la copia del *Los Angeles Times* che aveva tra le mani il giorno prima. Ed escluse che stesse soltanto guardando le fotografie. Sbirciava verso di lui con una attentissima discrezione. Non voleva farsene accorgere.

Ma era incuriosito da quell'uomo, da quella posizione un po' ieratica, assente, da quel silenzio assorto. Forse non era un professore, si disse Umber pensando a come in genere erano loquaci i suoi colleghi, pronti ad arguzie, malignità, pettegolezzi. Ma chi era allora? Uno sceneggiatore rimasto senza lavoro? Un medico in pensione? Un altro rotolato in California perché da nessuna parte del mondo era riuscito a metter radici? Fu così che gli venne in mente una domanda, nella sua genericità gli parve abbastanza legittima, e gliela fece.

"Lei abita da molto qui?" chiese, approfittando del

fatto che lo sconosciuto si era appena distolto dai suoi pensieri e aveva spostato lo sguardo dalla sua parte.

"Dipende da cosa intende lei per molto," rispose lo sconosciuto.

Umber fu colpito dalla saggezza di quelle parole. Gli disse subito: "Io sono qui da neppure un anno."

"Io da neppure un mese," aggiunse lo sconosciuto sorridendo. Scoprì una chiostra di denti perfettamente in ordine ma ingialliti come quelli dei grandi fumatori. "Mi chiamo Kloster."

Umber si chiese come aveva potuto sbagliare di tanto. Era tedesco, un tipo che lui aveva giudicato asiatico senza alcun dubbio.

Ma l'altro, intravisto forse il suo stupore, continuo: "Sono il dottor Jamshid Kloster, sono nato in Germania da padre tedesco e madre iraniana, Jamilé, che Allah la benedica. Sono qui per continuare i miei studi, mi occupo del rapporto tra il tempo e la luce."

Umber era disorientato. Trovò indiscreto chiedergli se era mussulmano.

"Allora è un professore?"

"No, sono un ricercatore, non insegno."

Il disorientamento di Umber divenne ancora maggiore. Un ricercatore. Perché allora se ne stava su quella panchina invece di essere in un laboratorio, perché non aveva una cartella di libri e plichi con sé, ma soltanto una sacca di tela da cui, poggiata com'era sulla panchina, spuntavano il collo di una bottiglia d'acqua minerale e una copia spiegazzata del *Los Angeles Times*?

***

Se non un'amicizia, tra Umberto Umber e Jamshid Kloster nacque almeno una consuetudine. Si trovavano al mattino dopo colazione in riva al mare, e camminavano per un tratto di spiaggia insieme. Anche Umber ora portava con sé un bicchiere di caffè o una bottiglia d'acqua minerale, qualche volta anche muffin o dolci al cioccolato che sistematicamente offriva a Kloster, e Kloster rifiutava. Non parlavano di nulla di personale, di nulla che riguardasse il loro passato in Europa. Sembrava un tacito patto. Molto tacito. Ognuno dei due aveva declinato all'altro soltanto le generalità e la professione. Un tedesco di madre iraniana, un italiano che aveva insegnato in Francia, un ricercatore nel campo della fisica, un professore di letteratura comparata.

Ma chi li vedeva passeggiare sulla sabbia dalla indoratura pallida di Laguna Beach li poteva benissimo scambiare per nulla più che due tardi hippie, non importa da dove venuti, e invecchiati fedeli ai propri sogni. I loro discorsi vertevano prima di tutto su ciò che avevano appena letto sul *Los Angeles Times*. Non si soffermavano troppo sulla politica, anche se tutti e due erano sostenitori del nuovo presidente, Barack Hussein Obama, ne amavano i gesti, le espressioni, le idee e ne condividevano i primi provvedimenti per contrastare la crisi in cui l'America era sprofondata. Non si soffermavano neppure sulle condizioni dell'economia: soltanto commentavano ridendo che non si vedeva più una macchina americana in giro per l'America, che un paese in cui le città erano state progettate per farle percorrere in quattro ruote, con cinema, ristoranti e persino chiese dove si entrava in automobile, aveva mandato a gambe all'aria la propria industria automobilistica, e si doveva rifornire dai tedeschi e dai giapponesi, che aveva speso tante energie per sconfiggere nella Seconda Guerra Mondiale. Più volentieri, commentavano notizie di cronaca : mareggiate con onde gigantesche, incendi sulle colline, omicidi a Down Town e rapine sanguinose nelle ville di Beverly Hills, o le recensioni a film appena usciti, come l'ultimo di Clint Eastwood, e a romanzi appena usciti, come l'ultimo di Patricia Cornwell. Poi, man mano, il discorso finiva sui loro progetti in corso.

Umber raccontava delle lezioni che stava tenendo all'Università. Kloster si era presentato come un ricercatore nel campo della fisica. Forse era vero, forse lo era stato a Heidelberg o a Lipsia o chissà dove, ma ora i suoi centri di interesse si erano spostati, era tutto preso da domande che apparivano ad Umber molto strane e oscure. Qual era il rapporto tra Dio e la luce? Si poteva ottenere artificialmente una velocità più forte di quella della luce, che non esiste in natura? Si poteva fissare in una formula matematica la velocità del pensiero? Si poteva fare altrettanto con quella dello spirito? Qual era il rapporto tra la luce e il fuoco? Questo almeno fu presto chiaro a Umber, digiuno di scienza ma non di metodo: che Kloster ragionava piuttosto come un mago zoroastriano, uno sciamano pellerossa che come un ricercatore di una università, tedesca per di più.

E fu questo che aiutò Umber a superare ogni inibizione, a spogliarsi anche lui dei panni accademici, che non gli erano mai calzati a pennello, e a confessare un giorno qual era il suo massimo desiderio e la sua massima ossessione. Quando Kloster lo sentì parlare per la prima volta dei personaggi dei romanzi futuri, della volontà di conoscerli, si illuminò tutto in volto. Stava per dire qualcosa, era evidente, ma si trattenne. Per quel giorno quasi non parlò più, assorto, come se un pensiero martellasse nella sua testa. Ma il mattino dopo, appena vide arrivare Umber, posò il giornale aperto sulla panchina e gli si rivolse con un certo fare solenne, in cui Umber riconobbe fusi tra loro la serietà tedesca e l'orgoglio iraniano.

"Io posso farteli conoscere," disse Jamshid Kloster.

"Cosa?" rispose Umber.

"Non hai capito?"

"No, scusa," rispose Umber e si sedette vicino a lui, estraendo dal sacchetto un muffin e cominciando a sbocconcellarlo.

"Vedo che hai fame."

"Tu sei ascetico, per i miei gusti, ti accontenti del caffè e dell'acqua, che qui poi sono più o meno la stessa cosa."

"Io ti offro di realizzare il tuo desiderio, e tu mi stai a parlare di queste sciocchezze?"

"Continuo a non capire."

"Ascolta, allora. Mi hai detto che la tua ossessione sono i personaggi dei romanzi futuri, che tu non potrai conoscere, è vero?"

"Certo, dovrei vergognarmene, ma è così."

"E allora, io ti ripeto che posso farteli conoscere."

Jamshid Kloster aveva preso Umber per un braccio e

lo teneva stretto. Lo guardava fisso negli occhi, aveva pupille nerissime e le iridi dello stesso indefinibile colore dei denti. Sembravano occhi di uno che farnetica per la febbre.

"Tu puoi?" chiese Umber.

"Sì."

"E come? Come è possibile?"

"Aprendo la porta del tempo," rispose Kloster. Aveva una espressione contratta e nello stesso tempo calma, decisa. Umber si mise a ridere, poi ripeté:

"La porta del tempo? Com'è, a vetri, a soffietto, in legno massiccio…"

Kloster scosse la testa ed estrasse dalla tasca della giacca di velluto un piccolo specchio esagonale, non molto più grande di quello che le donne usano per ritoccare il trucco, lo puntò in modo che riflettesse i raggi del sole, forti quella mattina, e li guidò contro un frammento di pagina del giornale, lasciato cadere ai suoi piedi. Con un piccolo crepitio improvviso, il frammento di carta prese fuoco, bruciò, divenne cenere. A Umber, tutto ciò diede un tremito, un formicolio lungo la schiena. Aveva smesso di ridere. Si pentì del suo sarcasmo di prima. E ascoltò confuso quello che Jamshid Kloster gli disse:

"Come nello spazio si può catturare il fuoco dal sole, nel tempo si può catturare il futuro dal ciclo eterno delle cose. Tutto è già stato e tutto ritorna. Non si tratta di prevedere il futuro. Ma di spostarsi in esso."

Ci volle qualche giorno perché Umber si decidesse a tornare sull'argomento. Vedeva Kloster indifferente, propenso a restarsene in silenzio. Offeso, forse. Umber era sicuro di averlo urtato con quelle sue parole sarcastiche, le riteneva stupide, ora, ma alla fine perdonabili.

Così ritenne giusto di essere lui a chiederglielo, una mattina di vento, con l'azzurro del mare tormentato da lunghe ombre grigie di nuvole, che faceva quasi freddo e non c'era nessuno sulle panchine vicine alla loro, e ci si godeva come non mai il caldo di quel caffè brodoso dei bicchieri di carta.

"Tu dici che c'è un modo per spostarsi nel futuro?"

"C'è."

"Navi spaziali, fughe nelle galassie…"

"Niente di tutto questo."

"Ma è assurdo, a pensarci, è assurdo…"

"Se a te interessano i romanzi futuri, dovremo spostarci nelle biblioteche future."

"Come diavolo è possibile… come vuoi che…?"

"Dobbiamo aprire la porta che da una biblioteca di oggi dà su quelle a venire," lo interruppe Kloster.

"Ma che cosa vuol dire?"

"Esattamente quello che ho detto."

"Come si può, come fare per…"

"Quello è compito mio, fidati."

"Metti che io mi fidi."

"È importante…"

"E poi?"

"Dopo aver aperta la porta, dobbiamo viaggiare."

"Dobbiamo? Anche tu… ?" chiese Umber.

"Io preparerò il tuo viaggio, se decidi di farlo, verrò con te, per assisterti, soltanto per quello. Sai, io non sono molto interessato ai romanzi, e i personaggi che tu ami tanto me li dimentico subito. Amo la musica, molto di più."

"E non ti interessa sapere come sarà la musica del futuro?"

"La musica migliore è quella che scorre, dammi retta, è la musica di quello che succede, dicevano in Irlanda, e là di musica se ne intendono."

"Ma i personaggi dei romanzi…"

"Le biblioteche ne sono piene ora, e ne saranno piene anche nel futuro, non so come ma lo saranno."

"Conosceremo libri a venire?" chiese Umber.

"Proveremo."

"E di cosa abbiamo bisogno?"

"Ci servono una biblioteca, quattro specchi, e un bel tramonto."

"Tutto lì?" disse Umber riprendendo a ridere. Non sapeva se di gioia o di derisione: verso se stesso il suo desiderio di credere al suo nuovo amico.

***

Come biblioteca, Umber scelse quella della facoltà dove insegnava, che era una grande sala con ampie vetrate esposte a ovest, da cui, tirando le tende, certamente sarebbero passati i raggi del sole al tramonto. Dovette ottenere il permesso di restarvi oltre l'orario consentito. La bibliotecaria, che lo aveva in una certa simpatia perché italiano – capita anche questo di curioso a chi se ne va per il mondo dimenticandosi di esserlo – gli lasciò le chiavi con un sorriso di compiacimento che siglava un accordo, il Professor Umberto Umber avrebbe avuto accesso alla biblioteca anche dopo le ore consuete di apertura, vale a dire dalle 18 in poi, e, impegnandosi a chiudere per bene la porta principale e a depositare le chiavi nella cassetta delle lettere dell'alloggio dei custodi, poteva restare anche tutta la notte a lavorare come desiderava. La bibliotecaria non aveva certo idea di che lavoro si trattasse. E questo pensiero metteva allegria a Umber, una allegria malsana, quasi da malfattore, si sentiva il dottor Jekill durante la giornata di insegnamento, si preparava a diventare il signor Hyde dal tramonto in poi.

Arrivò la sera in cui avevano stabilito con Jamshid Kloster di incontrarsi in biblioteca. Umber aspettò che gli studenti e le studentesse se ne andassero. E infatti poco prima delle 18 si allontanarono, alla spicciolata, fuorché uno che rimase con i gomiti sul tavolo e un quaderno di appunti davanti. Umber era impaziente. Guardava quel suo allievo, perché era proprio uno studente del suo corso, il più bravo, quello che poneva sempre le domande più intelligenti, con una specie di odio. Perché si attardava tanto su quel volume di critica, forse di René Wellek, forse di Erich Auerbach, forse di Harold Bloom, che cosa vi cercava, che appunti prendeva? Possibile che la sua fosse una strategia attendista, che avesse intuito qualcosa di ciò che stava per avvenire tra quelle mura? A quel punto, Umber sarebbe stato capace di ucciderlo. Ma per fortuna lo studente si alzò poco dopo, passò davanti a lui per salutarlo ossequiosamente, se ne andò.

Umber, sulla porta, fece il cenno convenuto con il braccio. Furtivamente Jamshid Kloster entrò nella sala, subito guardandosi intorno per valutare dove sarebbero finiti i raggi dell'ultimo sole. Bisognava fare in fretta. Lo individuò presto, era su uno scaffale, il terzo ripiano a partire dal basso, tolse i volumi che occupavano quello spazio senza neppure guardarne i titoli, li ammonticchiò su un tavolo. Dalla sacca che aveva con sé estrasse quattro specchi esagonali, di dimensioni maggiori rispetto a quello che aveva usato per incendiare il pezzetto di giornale, e li piazzò contro la parete a coprire lo spazio lasciato libero. Umber seguiva le sue mosse in preda allo sconcerto. Kloster si muoveva con decisione, ma anche con calma. Sembrava sapere quello che faceva, anche se chiunque avrebbe giudicato quello che faceva assurdo.

Quando il sole tutto rosso fiamma si abbassò sull'orizzonte, i suoi raggi, attraverso la vetrata di cui Umber aveva scostato allo spasimo la tenda, andarono a picchiare contro quegli specchi disposti là in mezzo ai volumi. Il calcolo si era rivelato esatto. Un fascio di riflessi purpurei e dorati si irradiò da quel punto e si scompose e si frammentò in vortici. Kloster e Umber cercarono invano di sostenere con lo sguardo lo sfavillio balenante, accecante, da caleidoscopio che si sviluppava da quello scaffale tutt'intorno. Una nuvola dai contorni di fiamma occupò la sala. Umber si portò una mano sugli occhi, in silenzio.

Kloster sembrava in trance, era come se pronunciasse a fior di labbra mantra in una lingua di qualche civiltà lontana. Poi il sole scese, e i riflessi impallidirono, rientrarono come sciabole in foderi scuri, nella biblioteca posò una luce bluastra, statica, esaurita. Umber si mosse, stava per andare ad accendere i neon del soffitto. Kloster lo trattenne. Gli indicò una lampada da tavolo lontana. Gli disse che quella sarebbe bastata. Umber la raggiunse a premette l'interruttore, diffondeva una luce fioca, puntata sul ripiano del tavolo stesso. Se qualcuno del campus fosse passato, avrebbe potuto credere che il Professor Umberto Umber stava preparando con così gran scrupolo la sua prossima lezione. Invece stava ad ascoltare le farneticazioni di Jamshid Kloster, che non aveva neppure titoli per essere lì.

"Ora apriremo la porta," disse Kloster.

"La porta della sala?" chiese Umber, disorientato davvero, quasi impaurito.

"No, vieni…"

Kloster si avvicinò allo scaffale dove stavano al posto dei libri i quattro specchi. Umber lo seguì. E qui avvenne ciò che mai Umber si sarebbe aspettato. Kloster scostò dalla parete uno dei quattro specchi come se fosse una mattonella traballante, ma invece del muro, invece di quello che qualunque ragione, qualunque logica, qualunque esperienza avrebbe detto con sicurezza matematica, comparve un ampio esagono di luce azzurra come quella di uno schermo, un varco verso qualcosa di immateriale e di lontano, in cui Umber, dopo un po' di esitazione, tremando e con il cuore in gola, osò finalmente gettare lo sguardo. Era quella, dunque, la porta del tempo di cui Jamshid Kloster gli aveva parlato, e a cui lui aveva riservato all'inizio la sua ironia? Esisteva un varco nello spazio in cui il pensiero superava i confini della materia?

Umber era stato un modesto adepto di Cartesio, sino ad allora, e aveva creduto nella divisione tra *res cogitans* e *res extensa*. Ma di fronte a quello che stava vedendo ora, come regolarsi, a quale nuovo sapere ricorrere? L'apertura esagonale si scontornò e si allargò, e in essa cominciarono a comparire forme precise e riconoscibili, una piazza di città, viali alberati, il traffico delle automobili, rare e diverse da quelle in uso al presente, l'andirivieni di una folla variopinta e straripante, poi un palazzo in vetro, legno, acciaio, è lì che lo sguardo attonito di Umber e quello tesissimo di Kloster venivano guidati, l'interno appena vi entrarono lo riconobbero per quello di una biblioteca, che però non capirono quale fosse e in quale città, poteva essere Los Angeles come Atlanta, Bruxelles come Parigi, Atene come Alessandria d'Egitto. Per via di qualche dettaglio cui forse prestarono più attenzione del dovuto, tutti e due pensarono che poteva trattarsi della Biblioteca Nazionale, quella in quattro torri a forma di libro aperto voluta da Mitterrand a Parigi, o di quella inaugurata non molti anni prima ad Alessandria, dove era stata la più immensa e famosa tra le biblioteche dell'antichità. Ma non ne furono certi.

L'interno era arioso ma labirintico. C'erano molti tavoli, deserti, molti computer spenti. Doveva essere notte. Poi ne videro uno acceso. Un calendario all'angolo destro dello schermo segnava la data, 3-21-20 N.E, cui seguiva tra parentesi 2109, evidentemente dell'era cristiana. Al centro vi compariva una figura mitologica, simile a un Centauro, e sotto la scritta annunciava i romanzi che erano stati acquisiti di recente dalla biblioteca.

Se poi di questi romanzi esistessero copie cartacee o se tutto si dovesse leggere su quello schermo di computer, Umber e Kloster non ebbero neppure il tempo di chiederselo. Si erano sentiti risucchiare in quella biblioteca futura, ed ora vi erano in carne e ossa, era come se fossero passati per quella apertura e avessero viaggiato a una velocità sconosciuta sino al 2109, o 20 di qualche Nuova Era che fosse. Fu Kloster che ebbe il coraggio di cliccare su quella specie di centauro, e la prima copertina uscì. Raffigurava una donna seminuda e a terra, circondata da fiamme e da uomini che avevano l'espressione di persecutori. Il titolo era : *L'ultima cristiana*. Seguiva una breve presentazione. Dell'autore nessuno dei due si fissò in mente il nome. Umber lesse, con un piacere che lo stravolgeva, e lo immalinconiva come spesso il raggiungimento insperato di un sogno.

***

"Giustina France, orfana giovanissima di padre e di madre, è spinta da un uomo che l'ha circuita a praticare il mestiere della prostituta per le voglie dei tanti ricchi che arrivano nella sua città per turismo o per affari. Giustina è alta di statura, magra, un volto affilato, piace agli uomini per il suo sguardo febbrile e per la sfacciata sensualità con cui si concede. Ma Giustina cova altro in sé. Quel suo sguardo non è febbrile se non per il disgusto che ha di sé e degli altri, quella che sembra sfacciata sensualità è abbandono alla disperazione. Un giorno decide di fuggire da quell'uomo e dalla sua città.

"Porta con sé una bambina, Gloria, venduta dalla famiglia e prostituita nonostante i suoi dodici anni, ascoltando la sua richiesta di aiuto. La loro fuga è ardua, mille pericoli le insidiano. Respinte, ingannate, tradite da molti, le due si allontanano da ogni strada battuta. Giustina vede crescere dentro di sé un nuovo coraggio.

"Sempre più lontana da città e villaggi, si imbatte in un vecchio edificio a due piani, in rovina, abbandonato tra macerie e sterpaglie. Non può credere che qualcuno abiti lì. Vi entra insieme a Gloria, e vi trova, terrorizzati dal suo apparire, uomini e donne, pochi, tutti anziani, che da tempo vi si sono rinchiusi per sfuggire alle persecuzioni degli ultimi cristiani autorizzate dal Governo di quella parte del pianeta. Giustina France, accolta con generosità e pietà, soprattutto da una donna chiamata Sorella Angela, decide di restare con loro, mette una croce al collo, si dedica a una vita di preghiera.

"I suoi compagni sono vecchi, vivono nascosti, sanno che non potrebbero opporre resistenza se venissero scoperti dalla polizia e attaccati. Dopo un anno, Gloria non sopporta più quel clima di preghiera e di paura, e decide si andarsene. Lo fa di nascosto, una notte. Ora tutti si sentono in pericolo, Gloria potrebbe essere intercettata, venderli, svelare il loro nascondiglio. Giustina vorrebbe ripartire, cercare un rifugio più sicuro. Ma gli altri non hanno più le forze per seguirla. Allora anche lei resta, curando le loro malattie, occupandosi di tutte le loro necessità.

"Man mano, i suoi compagni e le sue compagne muoiono, affidando le loro anime a un Dio in cui sono rimasti gli unici in quella parte del pianeta a credere. Quando muore tra le sue braccia anche Sorella Angela, Giustina resta sola in quel rifugio. Sono passati anni, e Gloria torna. Di nuovo stanca del mondo che ha avuto intorno. Giustina è felice di rivederla.

"Ma, senza che Gloria se ne sia accorta, qualcuno l'ha seguita. Qualcuno ha visto le due donne abbracciarsi, e ha visto il bagliore di una croce al collo di una, e subito dopo il segno della croce che l'altra ha fatto con la sua mano, prima di entrare nel vecchio edificio in rovina. La polizia arriva e arrivano le ruspe. Viene appiccato il fuoco alle sterpaglie, il fuoco si diffonde, Gloria esce tossendo e viene colpita da una scarica di mitra. Giustina rimane nel vecchio edificio, di fronte a una croce di legno che sta bruciando, tra le fiamme che divampano dappertutto. Anche lei, l'ultima cristiana, sarà arsa nel rogo."

***

Il Professor Umberto Umber era commosso e preso da una agitazione incontrollabile. Lui, il modesto studioso, l'ultima ruota del carro accademico, adesso era in grado di parlare del personaggio di un romanzo che avrebbe visto la luce tra cento anni. Soprattutto, era in grado di pensare a Giustina France come a una sua conquista, favoleggiare su di lei, sulla sua doppia vita di prostituta e di martire, pensare se l'avrebbe aiutata a evitare il rogo, era certo che l'avrebbe aiutata, ma come?

Voleva abbracciare Kloster per il risultato conseguito. Ma l'atteggiamento sempre composto e riservato del suo compagno lo tratteneva. Ora Jamshid sembrava stanco. Umber temeva di vederlo da un momento all'altro andare a prendere i libri della pila poggiata sul tavolo per disporli nello scaffale, dove avrebbero richiuso quella finestra miracolosa. Ma Jamshid non lo fece. Evidentemente non era stanco, soltanto concentrato, assorto nel suo compito. Che non era ancora finito. Attraverso quella finestra aperta nel futuro, il viaggio poteva continuare, lui non sapeva quanto ma sentiva che poteva. Umber lo pregò di andare avanti. Di proseguire di un secolo, almeno.

E Kloster scostò un altro specchio. La galleria esagonale divenne più lunga. Loro due, rimanendo fermi dov'erano, erano come risucchiati all'interno di quella galleria con maggiore velocità. Si trovarono in una nuova biblioteca, gli interni erano diversi, anche gli schermi dei computer, erano più grandi, sospesi su steli sottili e a due facce, perfetti nella resa delle immagini. Il procedimento però era sempre lo stesso. Kloster cliccò sino ad arrivare a visualizzare la copertina e poi la presentazione di un romanzo tra quelli acquisiti dalla biblioteca negli ultimi mesi. Il calendario segnava 3-21-120 N.E. Il romanzo era scritto in una lingua non nota né a Umber né a Kloster, ma questi capì che si trattava di anglo-mandarino, una lingua nuova evidentemente molto diffusa sul pianeta in quel tempo. Per fortuna, la lingua in corso non aveva cancellato del tutto le altre, un po', pensò Umber, come l'euro aveva a lungo convissuto, almeno nelle indicazioni dei prezzi, con la lira o i franchi. Dunque Kloster azionò il convertitore, e l'operazione riuscì. Il testo uscì in inglese. Umber cominciò a leggere con attenzione spasmodica. Così era sintetizzato *John Wei, commissario capo*.

***

"John Wei era stato un eroe della guerra che andava avanti da anni e anni. Aveva partecipato a una campagna in Pakistan come conducente di carri armati del tipo Libellula ESS 101, che potevano trasformarsi in elicotteri e in anfibi. Aveva condotto un assalto vittorioso, e una volta che il suo carro era stato distrutto, continuò a combattere da fante, munito soltanto di un coltellaccio e di bombe a mano. Si raccontava che da solo avesse ucciso cinquantasei nemici. Richiamato in patria dopo essere stato ferito e aver passato settimane intere tra la vita e la morte, John Wei, un uomo ancora giovane, che si era ripreso con sorprendente vigoria, venne nominato commissario capo della Polizia della sua città, megalopoli di 59 milioni di abitanti. Le autorità pensavano così di compensare il suo eroismo in guerra. Ma John Wei, che aveva visto la morte in faccia, era stanco di uccidere e aveva paura di essere ucciso a sua volta. Quando sul porto della città, un porto sconfinato con 150 chilometri di banchine, un cargo con tutto il suo carico venne fatto esplodere, seminando vittime anche tra i marinai, toccò a John Wei coordinare le indagini.

"Il commissario capo intuì subito che la forza per compiere un attentato di quelle dimensioni non poteva che appartenere alla Compagnia del Drago Bianco, una associazione criminale che voleva impossessarsi del porto e gestirne i traffici. Non essendo riusciti nel loro intento, i capi della Compagnia del Drago Bianco avevano progettato quel sanguinoso avvertimento. Poi continuarono. Un altro cargo saltò in aria, poi fu alzato il tiro, venne fatta esplodere una fregata della Marina ormeggiata lì e con quindici militari semplici e tre ufficiali a bordo. Il timore era che la prossima vittima fosse una nave passeggeri, una di quelle nuove navi da crociera in grado di portare in giro per gli oceani sino a trentamila persone.

"John Wei doveva evitarlo, quello era il suo assillo di commissario capo. Intanto un altro fatto ne turbava i sonni, e questo in un'altra sfera della sua esistenza. Si era innamorato di una delle sue sottoposte, una commissaria bionda e scattante, Jasmine Gard, irresistibile ai suoi occhi, ma sapeva che la legge gli avrebbe impedito di sposarla proprio perché sua sottoposta, e temeva che alla minima dichiarazione del suo innamoramento lei avrebbe potuto trascinarlo nella vergogna di fronte al TSCSS, il Tribunale Speciale dei Comportamenti Sentimentali e Sessuali, severissimo e temutissimo. Viveva dunque in silenzio questa passione.

"E dirigeva le indagini e la lotta contro la Compagnia del Drago Bianco con cupa, compressa energia. Dovendo infiltrare un agente nella Compagnia, sceglie la commissaria Jasmine Gard. Non sa neppure lui se vuole allontanarla, togliersela di torno per cercare di dimenticarla, con il rischio di farla morire, o se vuole offrirle una grande, irripetibile occasione per un avanzamento di carriera. L'operazione non riesce, Jasmine Gard è scoperta, torturata e uccisa.

"Solo più che mai, disperato, nemico anche di se stesso, John Wei ricomincia la sua lotta. È come se dovesse vendicarsi. E' come una nuova guerra, più terribile di quella che ha combattuto da giovane. Il porto continua ad essere insanguinato. Il commissario capo John Wei scopre che tra le Autorità della città c'è chi informa la Compagnia del Drago Bianco. Stana il corrotto, ma scopre via via nuove trame di collusione tra il potere e l'associazione criminale, sempre più vaste. Non riuscirà mai a troncarle del tutto, e lo sa. Allora, con il pensiero fisso a Jasmine Gard, si uccide sparandosi alla tempia seduto alla sua scrivania."

***

Kloster guardò l'orologio, non era sicuro di quanto tempo avessero ancora. Poi con decisione scostò il terzo specchio dei quattro che aveva posto sullo scaffale. Scivolarono silenziosi, rapidissimi lungo la galleria e si trovarono in una biblioteca del 220 N.E, che secondo rapidi calcoli doveva corrispondere al 2309 d C. Umber, sovraeccitato, tremando quasi, chiese di approfittarne, di leggere la presentazione di più romanzi. La biblioteca in cui si trovavano ora non aveva più niente della biblioteca come gli uomini l'hanno conosciuta nei secoli. Non c'erano tavoli, non c'erano sedie, soltanto lunghissime file di schermi piatti fissati alle pareti senza tastiere. Restando in piedi, si poggiava un dito sullo schermo e dallo schermo uscivano immagini astratte coloratissime, vorticose e indicazioni vocali su come procedere.

La lingua in cui quella voce metallica ma musicale si esprimeva fu all'inizio incomprensibile per Umber e Kloster. Questi andò avanti per diversi tentativi, puntando il proprio indice su tante icone dello schermo. Finalmente uscì una indicazione scritta, ed era in una lingua molto simile al tedesco. Ebbero una illuminazione retrospettiva, anche le indicazioni vocali erano in quel tedesco contaminato dal francese e da altre lingue nordiche, forse svedese, forse islandese: parlato, era stato molto più ostico da intendere che scritto. Kloster procedette. L'elenco delle ultime acquisizioni della biblioteca era lunga. Ne scelse una a caso. La copertina che uscì fu quella di *Chimera I regnò su di noi*.

***

"Una popolazione di incroci tra uomini e animali si era moltiplicata e espansa a partire da un errore nei laboratori segreti di eugenetica di una multinazionale con sede ad Amburgo, una popolazione incontrollabile dagli umani propriamente detti, che furono visti prima per un breve periodo come padri, e subito dopo come nemici da scacciare e distruggere. Gli uomini aquila e gli uomini calamaro (tra tante specie che vennero create, gli uomini farfalla, gli uomini topi, gli uomini serpenti, gli uomini rondine, gli uomini delfino, le cui femmine riproducevano alla perfezione nelle forme le antiche sirene, gli uomini cavallo, simili agli antichi centauri) furono le specie più intelligenti e più forti.

"I primi, capaci di volo e dotati di un becco feroce, occuparono campi e boschi, i secondi, anfibi, uomini dalla vita in su, ma con sei tentacoli al posto delle gambe, velocissimi e forniti di una terribile forza prensile, si impossessarono delle coste. Poi avanzarono verso le città, attaccandole dall'alto, insidiandone i tetti, e penetrandovi per ogni via d'acqua, fiumi, canali.

"Chimera (il suo numero di laboratorio era H6112MT) si era affermato sul campo come il loro condottiero, quello che sapeva tenere unite, alleate, le schiere degli uomini aquila e quelle degli uomini calamaro. Quando la loro forza di espansione si fermò, e si trovarono padroni di un territorio che comprendeva parte della Germania, dell'Olanda, del Belgio, della Francia, della Svizzera e dell'Italia, Chimera fu eletto re, e divenne Chimera I. La nuova capitale fu costruita sul Reno, una città di canali, in cui gli uomini calamari navigavano, e di torri alte e dal tetto largo, su cui gli uomini aquila vivevano pronti a spiccare il volo.

"Gli umani propriamente detti avevano perso tutto, vivevano da miseri schiavi. Chimera I, nonostante il suo istinto di guerriero, non era crudele. Aveva la conformazione di un uomo calamaro, ma il cervello e gli occhi di aquila. Delle debolezze umane in lui resisteva ben poco. Non aveva affetti, non provava né desideri né pietà.

Restio a formarsi una famiglia, adottò un piccolo degli uomini aquila e lo nominò suo erede. Sarebbe stato Chimera II, e avrebbe tenuto insieme il regno. Sui confini esterni, Chimera I non provocò guerre né accettò provocazioni.

"Ma sapeva che prima o poi sarebbe stato attaccato, che tutte le grandi potenze umane del Pianeta non avrebbero tollerato a lungo il suo potere su larga parte dell'Europa, e che le sue forze avrebbero stentato a respingere gli attacchi. Sul fronte interno, si trovò presto a dover domare insurrezioni. Erano gli umani che vivevano dentro i confini del suo impero, insofferenti della schiavitù in cui erano tenuti. Che mormoravano tra loro parole che Chimera I aveva proibito, democrazia, libertà, repubblica, e si proponevano di rovesciarlo. Regnava come se stesse sognando, e sentiva che nonostante il suo impegno di sovrano e la forza degli uomini- calamaro e degli uomini-aquila il sogno avrebbe anche potuto finire presto."

***

La frenesia di conoscere nuovi personaggi era sempre più acuta, il Professor Umber chiese a Kloster, quasi stringendo il suo polso, di puntare ancora l'indice sullo schermo, di esercitare quella piccolissima pressione, anche a caso. Venne fuori un'altra copertina. C'era un titolo in caratteri piccoli piccoli, *R66Dklein*, e uno strillo pubblicitario in caratteri cubitali, che diceva: *IL PRIMO ROMANZO SCRITTO DA UN ROBOT*. Era ancora in quel tedesco ibrido che Kloster in ogni caso era in grado di leggere e tradurre per Umber.

***

"R66Dklein è un robot di dimensioni piuttosto ridotte, di un bambino in sostanza, che racconta il suo essere a servizio degli umani, episodi della sua giornata, la sua partecipazione alla vita del padrone e della sua famiglia. R66Dklein descrive le sue giornate con precisione neutra, l'ora in cui entra in servizio, l'ora in cui prepara la colazione, l'ora in cui porta a spasso Wolfgang, il cane di casa. Non ha nessuna simpatia per il gatto Mozart, anche se non possiede le espressioni giuste per motivarlo. Racconta con artifici linguistici che sembrano preordinati, apparentemente senza nessuna concessione a dubbio, paura, angoscia.

"Ecco alcune delle sue prime righe, prima che il suo linguaggio diventi più fluido: "Ore 6,05 sveglio verifico stato mie batterie funzioni superiori articolazioni motilità – ore 6,15 apro finestre condizioni meteo controllate bel sole – ore 6,35 esercizi per migliorare mia forma, importante mia forma – ore 7,15 entro in cucina preparare colazione per padroni – ore 7,18 orzo nelle tazze, pane tostato con burro, formaggio fresco, frutta, tutto pronto – ore 7,19 Thor arriva a piedi nudi urla contro suo fratello piccolo Werner chiede una fetta di pane in più mette dita nel formaggio – ore 7,25 entra in cucina maledetto Mozart."

"E anche se racconta particolari buffi, si capisce che

lui ne ride soltanto con il permesso dei padroni umani. E anche se appare piuttosto incline alla allegria, si capisce che la gioia, come il dolore, del resto, non rientra nelle sue opzioni e nelle sue reazioni. Eppure la descrizione dei figli del suo padrone, Thor e Werner, bambini alti come lui, suoi compagni di gioco, ha qualcosa di fresco, e si avverte in essa una vicinanza ambigua alla natura degli umani.

"R66Dklein gioca perché è programmato per giocare. Imita Thor e Werner, ma in qualche momento arriva a sentirsi superiore a loro, per resistenza, per coerenza, per energia. Quando il suo padrone è richiamato con il grado di Ufficiale per la Grande Guerra Umana contro un oscuro regno popolato da creature mostruose, R66Dklein lo segue come scudiero. La sua partenza e il suo addio a Thor e Werner ("Ciao Thor Ciao Werner vado vado vado vado via via via via oh vado non vi vedo non vi vedo vado o no vado vado vado via o no no") ha momenti di strano calore, se non di vera commozione. La sua fedeltà al padrone umano durante diversi episodi bellici mostra qualcosa di generoso, che sarebbe improprio chiamare senso di devozione e di amicizia, ma che un po' vi assomiglia.

"R66Dklein si racconta con la sua intelligenza artificiale. Ma quello che colpisce è che nel raccontarsi sembra man mano crearsi da se stesso un abbozzo di anima. Mostra gelosia per un altro robot, scudiero di un Ufficiale amico del suo padrone, rimpiange la comodità della casa, prova orrore per le creature mostruose che gli umani combattono. Non arriva mai all' introspezione o alla esibizione di un ego, ma si vede che vi è vicino. Non riesce a ridere e a piangere col suo profilo di titanio e di cristallo, ma si vede che almeno nello scrivere vorrebbe arrivare a farlo. Il racconto si chiude con il suo ritorno a casa, il suo abbraccio con Thor e Werner, il suo primo litigio con il gatto Mozart e il suo pranzo a base di un olio lubrificante dal sapore di cioccolato."

***

Kloster fece segno a Umber che dovevano affrettarsi, e premette l'indice sullo schermo per fare apparire un' ultima copertina. Il titolo del nuovo romanzo comparve in caratteri arabi, che Umber non leggeva. Kloster, che dalla madre Jamilé aveva appreso il farsi, vi si orientava con sufficiente destrezza, e con una voce diversa, più calda, quasi quasi ispirata tradusse a Umber la presentazione del romanzo. Si intitolava *Saida è innamorata*.

***

"Saida, una donna di travolgente bellezza, ha vissuto la giovinezza all'epoca in cui le formazioni partigiane islamiche hanno impegnato a lungo le truppe dell' UCCA (Unione commerciale cinese americana) in Pakistan e in Afganistan, mentre formazioni cristiane le impegnavano in Africa e America del Sud. Di irriducibile fede islamica, il capo sempre coperto da un velo verde smeraldo, Saida ha manifestato un coraggio e una energia che l'hanno resa celebre tra tutte le formazioni combattenti. Anche quelle nemiche. Si raccontava spesso di lei. Erano nate su di lei leggende e anche canzoni. Se per i ribelli, anche per i cristiani, era forte come un'onda e bella come una rosa, per i nemici era una megera e una puttana, sulla cui testa pendeva una taglia di un milione di yuan-dollari di Hong Kong. Non si contavano i carri di tipo Pipistrello ESS 201 che aveva fatto esplodere, i duelli all'arma bianca vinti da lei contro soldati dell'esercito cino- americano, molto meglio equipaggiati e addestrati.

"Era una furia, Saida, e tutti la idolatravano, o la temevano o la disprezzavano, nessuno la amava. Di questo, lei si accorse soltanto dopo la vittoria, dopo che i ribelli con lei in testa entrarono in una città dominata sino allora dai nemici, che, stremati da distruzioni immense, alla fine si erano arresi. Furono momenti bui, di vendette, di sopraffazioni, di orrori. Nel resto del mondo la lotta continuava. Si capiva che i ribelli l'avrebbero continuata con ogni mezzo e a qualunque prezzo, anche a quello di distruggere la civiltà intera, pur di distruggere l'UCCA e il suo potere.

"Saida non voleva più saperne niente. Aveva deposto le armi. Era ancora bellissima, e finalmente anche lei se ne accorse. Aveva la pelle bruna come il miele di castagno, i capelli neri, gli occhi lunghi e del colore della giada, un corpo scattante ma anche morbido dove doveva essere morbido. Si innamorò, lei celebrata in tutto il mondo, di un giovane sconosciuto, semplice e dai lineamenti dolcissimi, che si guadagnava la vita raccontando antiche favole e leggende d'amore. Si trovò a dover affrontare la disapprovazione di tutti i suoi ex commilitoni e amici, che la richiamavano ai suoi doveri di combattente. Lo fece con l'energia di un tempo. Lottò contro tutti. Aveva fatto nascere leggende di sangue. Ora voleva vivere ascoltando leggende d'amore dalla bocca del giovane che avrebbe sposato."

**

Kloster si arrestò, guardò ancora l'orologio. Umber era in una specie di condizione estatica, per quel bottino così ricco, Giustina France, John Wei, Chimera I, R66Dklein, Saida, personaggi a venire di cui lui ora conosceva l'esistenza. Restava uno specchio da scostare. Kloster non sapeva sino a quando quella porta sarebbe rimasta aperta sulla galleria del futuro. La notte stava passando, la decifrazione di quelle lingue contaminate e ardue, il franco-tedesco-svedese, quello del romanzo sul re degli uomini chimerici, quello tutto contratto della prima autobiografia romanzata di un robot, l'arabo con influenze farsi, turche, urdu del romanzo su Saida avevano richiesto ore per Kloster, che doveva ogni tanto tirare il respiro e bere un sorso d'acqua. Bisognava fare presto. Umber gli stava gomito a gomito, impaziente.

"Ancora un passo, ti prego," mormorò Umber a Kloster.

"È l'ultimo."

"Lo vedo."

Kloster scostò così il quarto specchio. La galleria esagonale divenne ancora più grande, ma la luce che passava attraverso di essa sembrò subito affievolirsi. Non c'erano più le pareti di una biblioteca. Non c'era nessun computer, nessuno schermo. Si udiva il suono di una risacca. C'erano distese di sabbia e onde. Sentirono il vento soffiargli nelle orecchie, la sabbia finirgli negli occhi. I gabbiani e i corvi gridare volando in alto, sopra file di palme. Poi alla luce della luna comparve un sentiero che dalla spiaggia portava verso una collina verdissima. Tra gli alberi giganti, querce, pini, eucalipti, giunsero a una casa in pietra, alta come una torre, dalle finestre strette, che sembravano piuttosto delle feritoie. Passava una luce fioca da quelle finestre e usciva fumo dal camino.

Entrarono lentamente, attenti a dove mettevano i piedi. Nella penombra videro un camino acceso, in cui ardevano piccole fiamme. Poi uno scaffale su cui erano posati rotoli di un materiale simile alla carta, poi un tavolo. Sul tavolo, stava un foglio su cui era appuntata una data, V AE 2409 dopo Cristo, 1777 dall'Egira. E alcune parole, in latino. "Oggi io monaco (seguono lettere illeggibili) ho scoperto un racconto scritto in una lingua dalla lunga e gloriosa storia, oggi non più parlata, derivata a suo tempo dal latino. In esso racconto si trovano le seguenti strane vicende, da me così riassunte."

Umber e Kloster leggevano all'unisono. Mai più avrebbero pensato di finire nel latino, che entrambi traducevano senza difficoltà. Inoltre sembrava un latino facile, molto influenzato da lingue posteriori e barbare. Vernum Aequinox, il 21 di marzo, tra quattro secoli. Proseguirono, e la prima sorpresa del Professor Umberto Umber, italiano senza patria, scivolato in California, patria di tutti e di nessuno, fu quella di ritrovarsi di fronte alla propria lingua.

***

"In riva al mare, non lontano da qui, si incontrarono due uomini della stessa età, due uomini solitari e dominati da assurde passioni. Diventarono amici, o, in ogni modo, si instaurò tra loro una consuetudine, che li vide passeggiare ogni mattina e parlare dei loro progetti e dei loro sogni. Non erano più giovani. E sembrava che non fossero riusciti a stringere legami con niente di solido e reale al mondo. Era un'epoca in cui, del resto, non c'era più niente di solido e di reale nella nostra civiltà. Loro vivevano di fantasmi.

"Uomini di buoni studi, avevano virato verso il desiderio, verso la passione sfrenata, e gli anni che pesavano sulle loro spalle non li avevano aiutati a ravvedersi. Anzi, ricordando loro il tempo relativamente breve che gli restava da vivere, li avevano spinti con ancora più forza verso i loro miraggi. Uno osava sfidare le leggi della Luce e di Dio, l'altro, più frivolo, si unì a lui in quella sfida per un desiderio insensato, quello di conoscere i personaggi dei romanzi futuri. Un giorno, il primo propose al secondo di aprirgli la porta del tempo, di intraprendere insieme un viaggio folle nei secoli a venire, e quello sciaguratamente accettò…"

***

Umber e Kloster, sommersi da un'onda di terrore, non ebbero bisogno di andare avanti – avrebbero trovato i loro nomi, il loro appuntamento nella biblioteca al tramonto, i quattro specchi magici applicati contro la parete sullo scaffale e poi scostati come mattonelle traballanti per capire senza più ombra di dubbio, con un tremito che scavò loro lo stomaco e con un capogiro angoscioso, che quel racconto li riguardava, che aveva loro due come personaggi. E, quello che più li agghiacciò, che stava per svelargli il destino che li attendeva. Che cosa gli sarebbe successo, lì, in quel buio del 2409, un buio immenso appena rotto dai riflessi del fuoco, come dopo una apocalissi? Sarebbero riusciti a tornare indietro?

Un'altra ondata di terrore li sconvolse, fu una tempesta. Non riuscirono a leggere oltre. Né avrebbero voluto. Dal tremore, dal freddo che lo aveva assalito improvviso, il Professor Umberto Umber si mise a battere i denti, sembrava che non riuscisse più a smettere. Jamshid Kloster tossì, bevve in un sorso tutta l'acqua che restava nella bottiglia. Tutti e due si ritrassero, con uno scatto, a occhi chiusi. Poi Kloster fece i passi che lo dividevano dai volumi che aveva tolto dallo scaffale muovendosi con quella cauta progressione geometrica con cui si muovono gli astronauti nello spazio. Quando ebbe tra le mani quei volumi, tornò a rimetterli al loro posto. Si era riformato il muro, la sua opacità, la sua consistenza. Le estremità delle copertine rigide lo toccarono producendo un rumore sordo. Kloster controllò che i quattro specchi esagonali fossero nella sua sacca. Non se la mise a tracolla, la prese sottobraccio. In quel momento un filo della luce biancastra dell'alba che arrivava entrò attraverso le vetrate. Nella sala il buio si dissipò. Loro uscirono, correndo come ladri.

Umber, che continuava a battere i denti stava dimenticando di lasciare la chiave della biblioteca nella cassetta delle lettere dei custodi. Gli venne in mente che era già al volante. Non capì perché, ma soltanto quando tornò ed accese il motore della sua automobile si sentì un po' più al sicuro. Puntarono verso la passeggiata a mare di Laguna Beach. Non c'era nessun traffico, ci arrivarono in un attimo. Non scambiarono una parola. Entrambi avevano paura di quel silenzio e del loro stesso silenzio. Non erano ancora sicuri di essere tornati nel proprio tempo. Forse i due vecchi hippie, i due fedeli sognatori scivolati in California si erano sradicati persino da quello, e non lo avrebbero più riavuto. Quella strada d'asfalto, le quattro corsie, i semafori, certo, quei palazzi, quelle ville, certo, ma le onde del mare, la sabbia della spiaggia, il colore del cielo, non erano gli stessi che avrebbero visto se fossero rimasti ad attendere l'alba in quel futuro lontanissimo?

Che cosa gli sarebbe capitato, se fossero rimasti? E come quel monaco scrivano che loro non avevano visto, che forse dormiva nella stanzetta vicina, era venuto in possesso della loro storia? Chi l'aveva scritta? Ripassavano mentalmente in rassegna i personaggi che avevano incontrato, le loro vicende. Persecuzioni, mafie, cataclismi, esseri mostruosi, guerre. Ma anche dedizione, passione, eroismi, gioco, amore. Come ieri. Come sempre.

***

Cominciarono a star meglio quando il primo chiosco aprì e comperarono due bicchieri stracolmi di caffè. Umber, con le mani che gli tremavano, in difficoltà a estrarre una banconota dal portafoglio, prese anche un muffin, uno solo perché tanto sapeva che Kloster non ne avrebbe mangiato neppure quella mattina. Passeggiarono un po' sulla sabbia, bevendo, scaldandosi. Il sole se ne saliva dall'orizzonte prendendo energia e colore, un gran rosso fiamma che il mare appena increspato rifletteva.

Finalmente arrivò qualcuno. Due senzatetto che posarono una montagna di sacchetti neri tutti strappati e pieni di chissà cosa e si sdraiarono sull'erba dei giardini con la faccia dalla barba sporca e folta rivolta alla luce, come per lavarla. Poi la anziana signora in tuta bianca che occupò la sua panchina e si mise nella posizione del loto per meditare, per recitare mantra yoga, preghiere zen. Poi due ragazze dai pantaloni a vita bassa e dalle magliette strette e corte, con piercing che brillavano sull'ombelico, che si allontanarono sulla spiaggia abbracciate. Presto sarebbe passata correndo con la sua grazia discreta Diane Keaton, ci si poteva contare.

"Sai cosa penso?" chiese Umber. Soltanto da poco aveva smesso di battere i denti. Poté finalmente dare un morso al suo muffin.

"No," rispose Kloster, sorbendo con la cannuccia caffè dal grande bicchiere di carta.

"Il presente è bello," disse Umber, con la bocca piena.
"Davvero?" domandò Kloster, sorridendogli.

Laguna Beach – Sanremo, febbraio marzo 2009

AFTERWORD

A LIBRARY, FOUR MIRRORS,
AND A BEAUTIFUL SUNSET:
DECODING AND RE-ENCODING GIUSEPPE CONTE

The job of translation is a trial and error process, very similar to what happens in an oriental bazaar when you are buying a carpet. The merchant asks 100, you offer 10 and after an hour of bargaining you agree on 50.

Umberto Eco, "A Rose by Any Other Name"

Shortly after my arrival at Chapman University in 2008 as Musco Professor of Italian, my colleague, Dr. Mark Axelrod, Director of the John Fowles Center for Creative Writing, approached me with the opportunity of collaborating on the Italian Writers Series he was organizing for the Spring of 2009. Needless to say, I was enthusiastic. Actually, I was thrilled, especially after seeing the roster of writers that Mark had organized. In addition to providing some financial support, I was asked to introduce one of the writers, the Ligurian poet, novelist, critic, and columnist, Giuseppe Conte. Once more, I was overjoyed… and a little bit intimidated since, rather than deal with the early modern Italian authors I usually treat and from whom I am separated by centuries, I no longer had that comfortable chronological distance that would safeguard me from any possible discussion of misinterpretation. I now had the opportunity to meet and engage the author himself. Not just any author either, but a major contemporary poet and recent winner of coveted literary awards, the *Viareggio* Prize among them.

Although I had had meetings and conversations with some excellent Italian Canadian and Italian American authors (in addition to Italian Renaissance literature, I work on Italian immigration literature), and was thus not entirely new to the idea of engaging talented contemporary authors, this was my first important, formal event at Chapman University. While I was rather familiar with Giuseppe the poet, having read *L'ultimo aprile bianco* and *L'Oceano e il ragazzo* a number of years ago, this man was also the author of *La metafora barocca. Saggio sulle poetiche del Seicento*, an important study of Baroque literature, and a translator of a number of canonical English works. According to the arrangement, I was to introduce one of the most lauded contemporary Italian poets, translator, *and* the author of one of the most influential studies of the Baroque that I had cited in some of my academic work on sixteenth- and seventeenth-century Italian literature.

To add to my excitement (and anxiety), I discovered a mere couple of hours before Giuseppe's reading that I was to accompany the poet with a reading of some of his poems in English translation... but that he would decide which poems would be performed shortly before taking the podium. Luckily for me, Giuseppe is a kind, and conscientious man – the consummate gentleman, in fact – who seemed as interested in getting to know me as he was to discuss the reading. He indicated the few poems he was to read, discussed the English translation of a few key terms with me, smiled, and encouragingly said, "Andrà tutto bene."

Despite my nervousness at going into this reading cold, he was quite right for Mark afterwards mentioned how Giuseppe's reading was perhaps the highlight of the series that year. It was certainly the highlight of my first year at Chapman University. That particular event re-introduced me to Giuseppe's poems, and their translations. As further evidence of Giuseppe's generosity, shortly after his return to Italy, he sent Mark an original short story titled *I personaggi dei romanzi futuri* with the dedication, "Dovuto a Mark Axelrod." Once Mark and I read it, we knew it merited a special publication and thus was born the present translation with the accompanying original text. We can also thank Mark for the provocative English title. As the publisher, Michael Mirolla, perceptively noticed, only a bilingual edition would do for such a truly remarkable writer whose beautiful tale is the fruit of his experiences in southern California.

Without giving too much of the story away (for those readers who consult the *Afterword* before the actual story), I could not have wished for a better text on which to work. To say nothing of the thrill of being involved in the publication of an original, previously unpublished work with such a forward-looking publishing house that provides excellent editions of contemporary literature in a variety of languages, Giuseppe's story engages many of the themes and motifs of his poetry while at the same time explicitly treating time travel and translation.

The tale recounts Umberto Umber's all-consuming passion for reading the literature of the future, accompanied by his insightful guide, Jamshid Kloster. In Giuseppe's words, it is a tale of "A German with an Iranian mother; an Italian who had taught in France; a researcher in physics; a professor of comparative literature. Whoever saw them walking together on the pale golden sand of Laguna Beach would have easily mistaken them for aged hippies from who-knows- where, who grew old still following their dreams." While perhaps not immediately recognizable as intrepid heroes, they embark on an audacious literary quest that deserves attention.

While it may be very tempting to attempt to identify the character Umberto Umber with the author, one should not neglect Jamshid Kloster. Kloster, who "reasoned more like a Zoroastrian sorcerer, or an Indian shaman than a university researcher," reminds us that Giuseppe is also the co-founder of the literary movement "Mitomodernismo." This movement aims to revive modern society through a spiritual rebirth promoted by a recovery of basic human values as suggested by the myths of antiquity. For Giuseppe, this revitalizing quality of myth, affecting our language, life, and very souls, is as valid for the present as for the distant future.[1] That the mythical and shamanic are fundamental to his works should be lost on no one. Hence, Kloster the shaman-researcher incarnates the author's desires as much as Umber when he expresses many of the author's thoughts relating to the relevance of myth in our day.

"Just as in space one can capture fire from the sun, so in time one can capture the future from the eternal cycle of things. Everything has been and everything returns. It is not a question of seeing the future; rather, it is of travelling there."

As in the poem "Signore di Uomini" ("King of Men"), where the Palace of Mycenae with its great walls, bulls, and peacocks blend with the "Empire State, Pan Am, and Chrysler buildings,"[2] the myths still surround us and affect our everyday life, even if they have morphed into something new. This too may be seen in Giuseppe's March 1, 2009 newspaper article for *Il giornale* where, while commenting on his recent visit to California, he reflects on the indebtedness of modern society to American cinema, the contemporary source of myth. In this article, the proximity of the mechanical bull in the Saddle Ranch Chop House on the Sunset Strip to the Chateau Marmont that housed so many silver screen stars over the years, is the inspiration for a reflective glance at America's important role in the world's contemporary mythopoesis to conclude with the "certainty that myth and dream are still possible." It also shows that one can effectively portray good and evil, the just and the unjust, love and hate, and the beauty and terror of the universe on an illuminated screen in the inky darkness of a cinema.[3]

While the themes and images that Giuseppe conjures in *Angelina's Lips* certainly make for a very rewarding translation experience, even more so is the fact that so much of the story itself revolves around translation. That Umber and Kloster are two peculiar foreigners in the

United States who in practically the same breath comment on curious news items that appear in the *Los Angeles Times,* on the irony of seeing no American cars on streets full of drive-thru restaurants and churches, and who observe the differences between American and Italian coffee certainly stresses the importance of translating one culture to another. That they do this in English, which is their second or third language, again underlines the emphasis placed on translation. This, in turn, is further stressed by their dependence on interlinguistic interpretive skills in order to read the odd and often hybrid languages in which the sought-after novels are written in the libraries of the future.

Giuseppe Conte certainly seems sensitive to George Steiner's pronouncement that "each tongue – and there are no 'small' or lesser languages – construes a set of possible worlds and geographies of remembrance."[4] It is just so much more entertaining (and poignant) when the remembrance happens to be of the future in a work of fiction.

Written by someone of great sensitivity who is perhaps better known for his verse than his prose, Giuseppe's story contains numerous literary allusions that, with his deft and unique touch, resonate lyrically. The attempt to achieve a correct interlingual translation of this beautiful text from the source language of Italian to the target language of English is, naturally enough, fraught with potential pitfalls.[5] Despite certain similarities between Italian and English, particularly regarding certain verbs of motion and transitive verbs[6] (the story relates time travel, after all), the problem of equivalences inevitably arises.[7] The mutual transformation wrought by the act of translation is rendered thornier by the "fidelity *vs.* betrayal" syndrome – particularly acute in any decision regarding whether to "foreignize" or "domesticate" the source text in order to bring it closer to contemporary readers, or to become the true "cultural mediator" who guides the neophyte through the world of Italian literature and culture.[8]

In her study of translation between English and Italian, Cristiana Pugliese has stated that "it is important to establish first of all how relevant language variations are in the context of the source text and whether the lack of certain features will affect its appreciation on the part of the target text reader."[9] This sensitivity to the problems of register, idiolect, and sociolect between the two languages is particularly relevant to any consideration of the combination of references – whether oblique or explicit – to literary and cultural phenomena. As the protagonists of this story are both academics on a particularly intellectual quest, there are many linguistic similarities between them. Although fully aware that the act of translation "never gives back the source text unaltered,"[10] one often strives to balance the desired virtually invisible touch and the role of cultural mediator that, by means of lexical, syntactical, and grammatical choices, often colors the translated text in ideological or ethical shades that may tend to slightly vary it from the original.[11]

Although the entire translation project involved myriad choices, two examples should suffice in order to render the challenge and delight of decoding and re-encoding Giuseppe's tale. For example, when translating the reference to the military prowess of Saida in the fifth novel of the future, the original reads:

> Non si contavano *i carri di tipo Pipistrello* ESS 201 che aveva fatto esplodere, i duelli all'arma bianca vinti da lei contro soldati dell'esercito cino-americano, molto meglio equipaggiati e addestrati. [my emphasis]

I chose to render it in English with the following words:

> You couldn't count the number of *ESS 201 Winged Dragon tanks* that she'd blown up, or the close-quarter combats she'd won against the better-trained and better-armed soldiers of the Sino-American army. [my emphasis]

Although "pipistrello" is perfectly translatable as "bat" in English, a "bat-tank" would sound perhaps more comic book than I believe the author would certainly have meant. After a search through the various etymologies, histories, and heraldic references, I chose the connection between bats and winged dragons in Italian mythology and European heraldry. By referring to a dragon, I could allude to the myth of St. George and the 13th-century Ligurian chronicler Iacopo da Voragine's *Legenda Aurea* that, among other things in that rich work, refers to Saint Margaret the Virgin of Antioch who escapes from the belly of Satan (who had appeared as a dragon and swallowed her whole) still with the cross she bore in her hands.

Not only did this allow me to maintain the sense of

intimidation that such a war machine would convey, but it also allowed me to be true to the author's external and internal literary references, and the importance of the mythical. As a lexical substitution, this choice was grounded in relevant literary and cultural references that seemed to keep to the spirit of the story.

The second example is the reference to coffee. In stereotypically Italian fashion, the character Umber makes the following observation about North American coffee when witnessing Kloster drink it in a cup:

> "Tu sei ascetico, per i miei gusti, ti accontenti del *caffè* e dell'acqua, che qui poi sono più o meno la stessa cosa." [my emphasis]

This did not provide any particular challenge for translation:

> "You're an ascetic, in my opinion. You are content with *coffee* and water that are more or less the same thing here." [my emphasis]

However, in the fourth novel from the future, *R66Dklein*, "THE FIRST NOVEL WRITTEN BY A ROBOT," the original refers to R66Dklein preparing "orzo" (barley) for his masters at 7:18. This common coffee substitute in Italy has no cultural equivalent in English so it was merely replaced by the word "coffee" in the English translation. Lest someone believe this to be a trivial point, I refer to the importance Umberto Eco makes to the rendering of "coffee" in different languages. In *Experiences in Translation*, Eco declares that, while references to the plant can reveal reasonable synonyms, the resultant drink is not culturally equivalent from Italian to English. He writes: "Uttered in different countries, they produce different effects and they are used to refer to different habits. They produce different stories."[12] It is rather revealing that the bond between Umber and Kloster appears to be sealed by their shared appreciation of American coffee at the end of Giuseppe's story.

In conclusion, the translation of *I personaggi dei romanzi futuri* has been a complete pleasure and I hope that my enthusiasm is matched by the quality of the English text. Not only has this project afforded me the possibility of paying homage to such an obviously talented writer and gracious man, but also of collaborating with such other first-rate men of letters as Mark Axelrod of Chapman University, Pasquale Verdicchio of UCSD, and, of course, Michael Mirolla of Guernica Editions. I believe the timing to also be propitious since my completion of this essay coincides with my return from an inspiring conference on Translation Studies where I was in the company of such luminaries in the field as Gayatri Chakravorty Spivak and Lawrence Venuti.

Most importantly, with the year 2011 marking the sesquicentennials of the nation of Italy and Chapman University, this truly Italian and American work is a fitting tribute to both. On a personal level, I have been fortunate to reflect on this project at various times in four different and beautiful locations across numerous time zones in order to help bring this story and its message to a broader reading public. Somewhat like the story's protagonists, the magic of Umber's and Kloster's journey in the English version of Giuseppe's story has been realized with the help and inspiration of "a library, four mirrors, and a beautiful sunset."

Robert Buranello
Composed variously between Montreal, Wellington, Sydney, and Laguna Beach

NOTES

1. Giuseppe Conte, (1999), 20.
2._____ . (1997), 97.
3._____ . (2009) [online version]. Many of the passages of this article are developed and given further dimensions by the author in *Angelina's Lips*.
4. Steiner, xiv.
5. Jakobsen, 114.
6. See Dolores Ross, "Il ruolo della tipologia linguistica nello studio della traduzione" in Ulrych, 119-148.
7. Leonardi, 11.
8. Cristiana Pugliese, (2005) 12.
9. Ibid., 107. See also, Eco, (2001) 22.
10. Lawrence Venuti, "Translation, Empiricism, Ethics" in Feal, 74.
11. See Venuti (op. cit), and Gayatri Chakravorty Spivak, "Translating in a World of Languages" in Feal 35-43. Apel also agrees on the importance of the "creative" element in translation.
12. Eco, (2001) 18.

WORKS CONSULTED:

Apel, Friedmar. *Il manuale del traduttore letterario*. Trans. Gabriella Rovagnati. Milan: Guerini e Associati, 1993.

Conte, Giuseppe. *Il passaggio di Ermes. Riflessioni sul mito*. Milan: Ponte alle Grazie, 1999, 20.

_____ . *The Ocean and The Boy*. Trans. Laura Anna Stortoni. Hesperia Press, 1997, 97.

_____ . "Il simbolo di Hollywood? Un toro finto." *Il giornale*, 01 marzo, 2009. [online version]

Eco, Umberto. *Experiences in Translation*. Trans. Alistair McEwen. Toronto: Toronto UP, 2001.

_____ . "A Rose by Any Other Name." Trans. William Weaver. *Guardian Weekly*, January 16, 1994. [online version]

Feal, Rosemary G., ed. *Profession 2010. The Tasks of Translation in the Global Context*. New York: Modern Language Association, 2010.

Jakobsen, Roman. "On Linguistic Aspects of Translation" in

Lawrence Venuti, ed. *The Translation Studies Reader*. New York: Routledge, 2000, 113-118.

Leonardi, Vanessa. "Equivalence in Translation," *Translation Theory* 4:4 (October 2000) [online version].

Pugliese, Cristiana. *Translation as Cultural Transfer: Challenges and Constraints*. Rome: Aracne editrice, 2005.

Spivak, Gayatri Chakravorty. "Translation as Culture." *Parallax* 6;1 (2000) 13-24.

Steiner, George. *After Babel. Aspects of Language & Translation*. Oxford: Oxford UP, 1998 [1975].

Ulrych, Margherita, ed. *Tradurre, un approccio multidisciplinare*. Turin: UTET, 1997.

Giuseppe Conte was born in Imperia, Italy and studied at the University of Milan earning a degree in literature in 1968. Poetry books include *L'Ultimo aprile bianco* (*The Last White April*) and *L'Oceano e il Ragazzo*. *Le stagioni* (*The Seasons*) won the Montale Prize. The collection titled *Dialogo del poeta e del messaggero* (*Dialogue between the Poet and the Messenger*), includes the poetry suite *Democrazia* (*Democracy*) which touches on themes and tones of civil poetry. The last poetry volumes include *Canti d'Oriente e d'Occidente* (*Songs of the East and the West*), *Nuovi Canti* (*New Songs*) and *Ferite e rifioriture* (*Wounds and Reflorescences*), which won the Viareggio Prize. Novels include *Il terzo ufficiale* (*The Third Officer In Command*) which won the Hemingway Prize, and *La casa delle onde* (*The House of the Waves*), about the wreck in which Shelley was involved in 1822, and selected by the Strega Prize. Other writings include *L'adultera* (*The Adulteress*), a book of essays on travel and myth which won the Manzoni Prize, two opera librettos, three plays, two monumental anthologies, *La lirica d'Occidente* (*Western Lyric Poetry*) and *La poesia del mondo* (*The Poetry of the World*), and a travel book, *Terre del mito* (*Lands of myth*). He currently lives in Sanremo.

"Imagine the contours of an obsession. The distance between Angelina's lips and the contours of a Laguna Beach sunset is not great. *Angelina's Lips* is a story of the main character, Umberto Umber's, homonymal identity; a story of the search for what is not one's self. There are many ways to recount such a loss: live through the opportunity of homonymity (the same as anonymity?), or roll to the edges and corners of a continent. Southern California offers just such an opportunity, tucked on the edge of the Pacific (itself a contradiction) and, paradoxically, a terminus of sorts where life finds continuous renewal even if only on celluloid. As *Angelina's Lips* unfolds, the character Jamshid Kloster tells the protagonist Umber: 'If you're interested in future novels, we must travel to the libraries of the future.' The libraries of the future are the memories of the present, memories of travel, visitation, dialogue and observation, all of which accumulate their effect as they are translated beyond our own experiences and languages. The intimacy of a memory travels via its retelling, as Conte has done with his, and as Roberto Buranello has done in his excellent recounting of it in English." – Pasquale Verdicchio